SAUSAGES AND TRASH

Acknowledgements

My thanks to Simon Wallman-Girdlestone for his pedantic editing and correcting of the manuscript which challenged my patience and enhanced my creativity and saved the storyline; to The Royal College of Psychiatrists and The Maudsley Hospital, London, for insights into mental ill health; to Sam Smith for encouraging me to believe in myself as a writer; to Moniack Mhor and HUG for their support and encouragement; to Mairead Furlong who believes one day I will appear on breakfast television in just the way a friend should! To Sue Piper for her editorial skill and insight.

Jane Wallman-Girdlestone

SAUSAGES AND TRASH

Vanguard Press

VANGUARD PAPERBACK

© Copyright 2011
Jane Wallman-Girdlestone

The right of Jane Wallman-Girdlestone to be identified as author
of
this work has been asserted by her in accordance with the
Copyright, Designs and Patents Act 1988.

All Rights Reserved

No reproduction, copy or transmission of this publication
may be made without written permission.
No paragraph of this publication may be reproduced,
copied or transmitted save with the written permission of the
publisher, or in accordance with the provisions
of the Copyright Act 1956 (as amended).

Any person who commits any unauthorised act in relation to
this publication may be liable to criminal
prosecution and civil claims for damages.

A CIP catalogue record for this title is
available from the British Library.

ISBN 978 1 843866 6 71

Vanguard Press is an imprint of
Pegasus Elliot MacKenzie Publishers Ltd.
www.pegasuspublishers.com

First Published in 2011

Vanguard Press
Sheraton House Castle Park
Cambridge England

Printed & Bound in Great Britain

For Simon, Betty, Nikki, Phil, Anna and Zach, with my love and appreciation.

HMP Starling

12th February

Dear Natalie & Matthew,

It seems as though your mum and I aren't so different after all when push comes to shove. Here I am writing to you and asking you to do something important for me, just as we both felt we had to do something important for your mum.

I have been through the wringer. But there, you will know that for yourself by the time you read this. You know I have come to believe that all things work out for the best in the end. Mark my words.

I am sorry we have not, at the time I'm writing to you, been reconciled in person. I do understand your Dad's wishes and maybe it is for the best that you are given your space and allowed to grow up without all the baggage of my 'misdemeanours' being thrown at you. I have respected your Dad's wishes. But don't think I have been happy with that, I've missed you both.

Remember Bella at Geraldine's - I know she would love a special game and play if you are ever in the area. Geraldine is a good person to talk to if you ever want to know about me. I have included her address in this file, which I am leaving with my solicitor.

I have asked the solicitor to read this file and to help you to make sense, when you are ready, of who I am and why I did what I did. If you were to ask me now, I would say that the campaign I began was one of the main reasons I was put on the planet - that and to give birth to your mum.

If you do ever read this, I know you will decide what's for the best for you. My story lives on in your telling.

I have been so sorry not to be able to be with you as you have grown. But I hope whatever you are doing - these papers help you to realise that in these last years of my life I have been able to be *comfortably and fully me. More me than ever before.*

I have genuinely no regrets Natalie, Matthew.

I love you both and I am very, very proud to be your Grandma.

With my love,

Grandma Babs

XX

Defender

Global

Read today's paper – Jobs   Search

Defender Global   **The Defender**

Home   UK   Audio   World   News
   Now   Blogs   Search   Arts   Media

Put that in your mouth and eat it

Brian Ansell
Monday May 19th
The Defender

Brayston has become a hot potato for the supermarket chain *Worth It.* The talk of this small market town that is no stranger to protest (Nuclear power protester Damien Brakespeare lives here) is no longer about the teenagers in the square on a Saturday night or the ostrich steaks at the popular Farmers' Market. Forget "Angry of Tonbridge Wells", Brayston residents are in revolt.

Just a few months ago, people of a certain seniority could be seen at the checkout of the High Street and the out of town hyper-store, methodically removing the packaging from their grocery items before paying. *The Women's Federation* campaign, launched nationally, caught the imagination of residents appalled by the wastage caused by the excessive packaging demanded by the country's largest supermarket chain. They were determined revolutionaries joining the many across the country forcing the nation's habits to change and witnessing our country's huge landfill sites becoming a thing of the past.

Now the campaign has re-branded itself and developed an *organic* life of its own. Somebody is placing messages to consumers inside the food packaging of perishable items. Five customers have so far complained to *Worth It* in Brayston alone regarding the sausages, burgers, sausage rolls and scotch eggs they have purchased. Each packet revealed a sinister, hand printed warning not to eat the food as it contained additives and preservatives that kill.

Violet Mawcroft, 77, a regular customer at *Worth It: One Stop*, the small branch in the High Street of the multi-million pound chain said, "I am frightened to buy any meat or vegetables here now just in case it has poison in it. You don't know who's doing it and why. It could be Al-Qaeda."

John, 24, a local estate agent: "The person who did this is nuts. *Worth It* helps keep Brayston on the map. I've got a sausage roll for lunch and no secret message. If there was any kind of health problem with the food, *Worth It* wouldn't be allowed to sell it, would they?"

That is, of course, the question. There is a growing body of opinion which suggests that there is a strong link between mass produced, convenience foods and a higher risk of cancer and heart disease. The cause is the high level of chemical additives and preservatives, not to mention hydrogenated fats, that are used to make the foods last longer on the shelf and taste and look more palatable to us as consumers.

It can't be right though that a person or the people doing this are simply trying to draw our attention to the health risks? Surely there must be more to it than this?

Worth It store manager, Ian Fletcher, 31: "*Worth It* take very seriously any offence involving tampering with goods that are on sale in our stores. Our food is of the highest quality and is packed to maintain freshness. If any customer finds a tampered-with pack please return it to the store with your receipt and we will issue a refund. This matter has been referred to the police."

Brayston Police Chief, Inspector Alan Molyneux, was unavailable to comment.

Canalside Cottage,
Chandler's Lane,
Wynleigh,
Brayston BY3 2PG
Tuesday 12th September

My Dear Babs,

I haven't written before because I just haven't had the first idea what I ought to say. I felt at a complete loss about how to make a start, but I want you to be sure that I never doubted for a moment that, once I could clear my head of all those mixed up thoughts, I would want nothing more than to be in touch and to support in whatever way I can. I don't think I feel responsible in any way now for what has happened, but I do think I am involved.

I will not judge you, my dear, you did what you felt you had to do. I did think however that I should write to express my concern for you and to remind you how much you have meant to me over these last years. We may not go back into the dim and distant past but I have found such a good friend in you. We had some wonderfully happy times together. I hope you do not forget this during, what I am convinced will be, personally, frightfully challenging times.

I cannot condone what you have done. I think you know me well enough to know that. I cannot deny that I have had a rather difficult time particularly with the press regarding the nature of our friendship. It was utterly humiliating to be implicated in your actions – but it was my pride that was injured and not the real me or my friendship with you.

I understand from the news that you are in hospital undergoing tests. I have been assured that this will reach you. I do so hope so. I hope it's nothing serious.

I have continued with the garden today. It was while I was dead-heading that I had the strongest of impulses to sit down and write – here and now. Not be put off by my own sense of inadequacy.

So here I am sitting on that old wooden chair at the little iron table by the forsythia with a mug of coffee, enjoying the warm morning sun. I can hear a very vocal blue tit or similar and Toddy has already come to say hello – and ask for another sachet of food. Greedy puss. Bella is asleep at my feet, having polished off a tennis ball this morning! SHE IS SUCH A JOY. She sends a lovely big lick, a tail wag and a cuddle. I know she misses you. We both do.

Some things do stay the same, although I imagine that may be hard to believe at this moment.

I was worried I wouldn't know what to say, so I have tried to imagine us sitting together here as we used to – and I have tried to write as honestly as I would speak to you. I feel I owe you this.

The sermon on Sunday was all about standing with those who are on the edge and who are vulnerable, as they are very special to God. I have become slightly paranoid of late and wondered if the new curate was referring to you, but I think he was talking very generally.

I couldn't help but think about you and I felt ashamed that I have been such a fair-weather friend. You deserve so much better than that dear Babs, so much better.

Yesterday I was on duty at the charity shop as usual. It was quiet and there are only so many shelves to dust! The papers are thankfully no longer full of you – except for the local paper who seem to be attributing all sorts of other unsolved 'happenings' to you. I am deeply dismayed by the prejudicial nature of this publicity, but I am satisfied that you have a first-rate solicitor and that 'all manner of things will be well'.

We must both hold on to that thought, I think. I have seen the Rector several times since your arrest. She has been my rock, listening to my concerns and reassuring me that you will be looked after. In a sense, she has nudged me to trust my own instincts about what to do and when. So this letter is me doing what I believe is right and supporting a person I care for.

There, I have said it – and seeing it written there I feel it is right. I am here for you and you are my friend. I am sure this wasn't what we envisaged when we met all those months ago – but what is done is done. Friendship is what I believe matters now. My dear, do take care of yourself. You are very much in my prayers and thoughts. I will write again very soon.

With love,
Geraldine

EDITED TRANSCRIPT OF PSYCHOTHERAPY SESSION ONE

Name: Barbara Drapper
Hospital Number: 9365286673
DOB: 23.03.44
Consultant: Dr Ishmael Maharinjiti
Psychotherapist: Jessie Arkwright

Extracts from Session One

Jessie: Can you tell me a little about how you got started in campaigning?

Babs: There was never a Eureka moment as such, no. I was more caught out one day when I arrived at the checkout and started to put my shopping on the belt. It was ridiculous. Whichever which way I looked at it, I could not go on playing Little Mrs Victim any more. It was down to me. There was more *I* could do. I started to sort of fizz inside. Not explode. I didn't feel angry. Not then. More determined. I'd found a reason to carry on I suppose.

I watched the girl exchange a look with this older woman on the next till. John, one of the friendly security guards was at my shoulder. The girl had been clever, I hadn't seen her tip him the wink. I realised then that my face was known.

Jessie: How did that make you feel?

Babs: Funny feeling, yes. Odd. A bit sinking; a bit humiliating at the same time. I grabbed at my frozen foods. I always start with them. John reached for a fresh carrier.

He made his usual little joke.

I suppose it was all a bit of a laugh to him. It must be as dull as ditchwater working the front door all morning.

I always had the feeling he thought I had lost the plot.

I remember quickly getting the packaging off each of the things and shoving it into the bag John held open.

My mind was racing. He felt a long way away, but I could smell his sweat and see the little scratches on his hand. I wondered if he'd been pruning something or had just got a kitten. Marmalade, my daughter's cat, scratched like that when he was a tiddler. I wanted to say that he needed to bathe the infected area in some antiseptic and watch it a little. Check his tetanus was up to date. It looked as though it might be deep. I dropped the wrapper from the mince and put it in my cool bag. Then the plastic from the veg and fruit. I didn't dare look up. I couldn't catch my breath. Not properly. I knew the queue was restless. Nothing was said, but you could sense it. Just like walking into a waiting room when the doctor's running very late. Everyone fidgets more.

Jessie: How did you feel at the till?

Babs: I remember I felt disappointment. I was whacked. I wanted to get out of there PDQ. It wasn't me somehow.

I sat for half an hour or so in the car.

Jessie: You care a lot about the environment?

Babs: …Climate change, all that environmental guff was filling the newspapers and making the headlines on telly. Documentaries coming out of your ears about the changing planet and the effect cutting down the rain forest was having. You had to be blind, deaf and dumb not to pick up on it and have some sort of a view. I'm not saying I have overly much sympathy for eco-warriors per se. Most of them could use a hot bath, a hair cut, not to mention a nit comb – and they would do well to think about how they could help make the planet a better place by doing an honest day's work. Can't deny that they make their point loud and clear though. They get coverage. That's all that matters these days, isn't it? Media seems to love them. At the time it set me thinking.

Jessie: Thinking?

Babs: I think it was the Women's Federation who first started the 'lobby your supermarket campaign'. I've taken *The Defender* for years as they are good on health. They did a two-page spread called "Women with a Mission". I cut it out and kept it on the notice board in the kitchen for ages. I liked the fact that the women looked so ordinary in the photo. They had never done anything like it before. None of them. Apart from something about baby milk. I shared their concern. I wanted to get the big chains to be more responsible.

Jessie: You joined them?

Babs: I've never been a joiner of things – but there was something about them which got me going; captured my imagination I suppose. They rang true. I've always hated putting all my rubbish out for the bin men. I couldn't believe I could actually produce that much in a week, especially since it's been just me; me on my own. Then there was all that scare-mongering in the press about charging people to empty their wheelie and putting a microchip inside it to find out what you threw away. Well, I thought this was a good way to fight back. We shouldn't take this sort of thing lying down, not in my view at least. It seemed simple and not too, well, naughty. A letter here and a letter there. Just the cost of time and a few stamps really. I felt quite proud to have something to do which felt – well – significant. Important in its own way.

Jessie: Fight back?

Babs: ...It's true. I've always thought there's something basically very unfair about supermarkets. Where have all the greengrocers gone? Corner shops? Old-fashioned hardware stores and those stationers that stocked ones and twos of things? I'd not thought till then that we could be telling the supermarkets what we want, rather than them telling us what we should buy. What gives them the right to trick us into buying the stuff they want to off-load and then make billions of pounds worth of profit off the back of us acting like a flock of sheep? That's before you even start to get your head round what it all does to the planet. Yes, I do get hot under the collar. It does matter.

Jessie: It does matter.

Babs: The more I read about the Women's Federation campaign – less packaging, more responsible behaviour from the big supermarkets – that sort of thing – the more I knew I wanted to help. I really wanted to. What did it matter if I was laughed at. I had got off my backside and decided it was about time I did something.

Jessie: How did that make you feel?

Babs: I don't like being laughed at. I really don't. Never. Ever.

The Women's Federation wanted people to be part of a two-pronged attack. They were lobbying government people and the supermarket bosses.

Their campaign was all about "changing people's perceptions" they said. Reminded me of the bits and pieces we'd get through from time to time at the practice about the changes in the NHS. It took me a while to work out that they were only right up to a point.

Jessie: Up to what point, Babs?

Babs: Well, I wouldn't ask a cat to mind my pet mouse. You don't waste time with the government who are hand in glove with the big boys in the business world. It stands to reason. One depends on the other. The government wants the tax; wants people spending and borrowing more, especially now we are all in a recession – and so do the supermarket giants. Keeps everyone needing everyone else and in between times, when the back-scratching stops, there's some big hand-outs all round for those that are in the right place at the right time.

Jessie: How do you mean, Babs?

Babs: There was the minister of the environment on the late news. I don't usually watch, but I couldn't settle that night. All the heavy stuff would soon have me yawning and heading back to bed I thought. I suspect to this day Stephen Ballityne was on the make and just got 'hoisted on his own petard', as Derek would have said in the heat of the lights and the excitement of doing a programme. He certainly lost the plot all right. Let his mouth run away from his head! Even had me glued to the screen just to see what he'd say next! Do you remember the headlines? He had to resign a week later! Good.

He was a hypocrite. Director of one of those consortiums that own a whole load of high street shops! Called on shoppers to teach the supermarkets a lesson; no invested interest there then! Asked us all to be responsible environmentalists and leave all wasteful packaging at the till. Well, I couldn't believe my ears. It was certainly one better than writing to my local supermarket and asking them very nicely to see the error of their ways.

The papers had a field day. I cut out the one that was my favourite:

"It's not often that a member of the government recommends direct action."

Jessie: Can you tell me anything about who else was involved?

Babs: There were loads of us. Across the country. When you added us all up. It started with just a few odds and bods, but you didn't need to be an astrologer to see what was going on. People soon got the hang of it. I'd check out each evening on the Net the stories of the day. Got linked with others through PeopleDirect, the online network site. But mostly it was the locals who carried articles. I printed some stuff out and kept it in a folder. Then the box files. They were like an inspiration; encouragement. 'You are not alone, girl'.

Jessie: When did you become active?

Babs: With the packaging mallarky? After I saw the headline: "The Public haven't been this mad since war was declared." I started after I read that. I thought I was the only one doing it at my *Worth It* to begin with. But I needn't have worried. It was just that it felt like weeks before I even caught a glimpse of my first stray piece of cellophane left by a customer. I suppose the staff had been briefed to clear up as quickly as they could after an 'incident'. I expect that's what it was.

Jessie: How did you feel when you were leaving the packaging by the till?

Babs: … Yes I suppose I had got quite good at looking all calm and collected but I was just like a duck swimming upstream, paddling hard under the surface. I'd put on my professional face and try and relax my body, a trick I learnt from a ward sister years ago. She said I looked like a frightened, jumpy rabbit around patients who were dying. Just focus on the here and now and not on what might be made of things. You have to do that a lot when you see patients. Forget what's going on in your own life and just focus on what's right in front of your eyes; how they look; how they sound; what they tell you.

…

Jessie: Geraldine?

Babs: Geraldine was the encouragement I needed. I'd been very tempted to give up. I was feeling a bit indignant actually, finishing off packing my one bag of naked groceries and shoving all the packaging into two further *recycling* bags to take to the car park bins, when for some reason I looked up. Maybe a little one had cried out or maybe I just looked up because I sort of needed to take in more air in the middle of the operation, I don't remember.

Jessie: You sound as though you felt tense?

Babs: Two aisles down was a grey-haired woman, similar height but a great deal slimmer, much more elegant than me, ripping packaging off her stuff as though her life depended on it. Her face was red and for a second I was totally caught up in her speed and determination. It was like watching an Olympic swimmer go past you when you're bopping along in the slow lane. She looked pretty angry. My heart leapt.

Jessie: Your heart leapt?

Babs: Maybe I was nosey. I didn't feel like I was interfering at the time. I couldn't help myself. I came to a standstill just by the trolley she was packing. Before I could stop myself I'd asked her if she wanted a hand.

Jessie: Was Geraldine OK about that?

Babs: There might have been a split second of suspicion, but she seemed to have clocked my bags of cardboard and paper, then my shopping and decided I wasn't taking the mickey. Her frown broke into one of the broadest grins I have ever seen. She handed me the cardboard in her hands and I had my work cut out, I can tell you, trying to sort the rubbish into different piles as she ripped the covers off and packed.

We didn't talk much. We ended up somehow sitting opposite each other in the restaurant drinking café latté. The rest is history. Geraldine is a good friend.

Jessie: Geraldine is a good friend.

Babs: Of course. She is important to me. We never consciously campaigned together. The papers got all that stuff wrong and I know she felt disrespected over that. As though I had in some way let her down. It wasn't true.

We quickly realised that we didn't normally shop at the same time – or even on the same day in the week. It was coincidence we'd both found ourselves in the store on that day. Some people would say that was fate, wouldn't they? Or Divine intervention. I gave up on all that years back. Anyway it seemed as though in no time we had said, without being able to quite put your finger on how, that we both agreed we were going to be shopping at this sort of time next week.

Geraldine and I have a fair bit in common. Both retired. I guessed she was two or three years older than me. I felt a real air of anticipation that day. I hadn't realised that standing up for what you believe in could be so – I don't know – invigorating. I felt a different person when I walked back to the car.

Jessie: Geraldine gave you confidence.

Babs: I don't know. We never really discussed that first meeting, but I thought about her off and on all week. I kept catching myself imagining us both reaching the check-out in next door aisles at the same moment and both taking off our packaging at tortoise-like speeds. Aware the other is right there, close by.

Jessie: Did you find it exciting Babs?

Babs: Geraldine is more into supporting and encouraging. In one daydream I had a TV reporter and a camera crew in on it. It didn't work too well. I got frustrated and I lost Geraldine when they asked us to do it all again! Sounds daft now, but I saw us as sort of heroines, a bit like the suffragettes. People would smile and applaud as we went about the business of saving the planet in the supermarket queue! I'd have even had the canned store music playing "Feed the World" loudly in the background. My Derek always said I had 'my head in the clouds'. I can be as daft as a brush.

Tuesday finally came. When I did spot her in the shop it was all a bit furtive and a terrible anti-climax. You'd have thought we were shoplifters the way we carried on! I had a cold. Geraldine looked that anxious that I was sure she'd spent the week having second thoughts. I should have trusted her with my mobile number from the start – she'd have probably called the whole thing off. Anyhow, the security bods spotted us pretty much from the off and gave us what felt like their undivided attention. The second we had finished 'the deed', we were shoved out of the store in no uncertain terms. Everyone in the car park watched. That's how it felt.

Jessie: Did that feel difficult?

Babs: Geraldine said she had to rush off. I tried to persuade her to come for a coffee at Luigi's Wholefoods. She said she didn't know it. Later she told me she had lied and she even went and sat in there the following week to see if I'd turn up. I was wiped-out.

Jessie: You felt tired?

Babs: It was an important lesson learnt. It took too much of my emotional energy to be responsible in any way – even if it was only in my imagination – for another person. Whatever I was going to do, I would have to get used to being alone.

Canalside Cottage,
Chandler's Lane,
Wynleigh,
Brayston BY3 2PG

My Dear Babs,

Thank you so much for your swift reply. In so many ways you have put my mind at rest although I am still terribly concerned for you.

I do understand and empathise with your reasons for taking the actions you did, but I would be lying to you, my dear friend, if I said I was comfortable about the lengths you went to and their inevitable outcomes.

I can remember that it did cross my mind at the time that it was quite a major change of plan, when you told me you were off to see the UK on an extended painting holiday. We'd talked more than once about my various sojourns and I thought I was in no doubt that your home was very much your castle and woe betide anyone who suggested otherwise, particularly if it involved going away.

I must admit that initially I was more than a little envious that you had taken such a bold decision. Indeed I wished I had half the nous. I would have loved to have planned and gone on a not dissimilar expedition. I fleetingly considered suggesting I came with you for part of the way just to be a companion and fellow dabbler with the watercolours, but there was something about the way you talked with such animation and determination which made me realise pretty quickly this was a very personal quest.

My enthusiasm was deflated however when I realised you intended to travel in a camper van! So right for one – but I think it would have tried the patience of even the most amicable of friends! I can remember how thrilled you were when you first showed me round your latest purchase. I am sorry I was so sceptical. I have an old woman's caution – and I was genuinely worried about how you would cope – not with the day to day but with the loneliness or if anything untoward happened. As things turned out I needn't have had a second's concern.

The camper van was so dinky. I thought calling it Rocinante was a stroke of genius although you did no tilting at windmills!!!! It couldn't have been cosier, could it? You really did have all mod cons – particularly once you had the laptop, the solar panels and the satellite dish. Maybe I should have been more observant and asked more questions. Perhaps it was wise I didn't!!!???

I loved the fact that Bella had what amounted to her own berth in the front seat. That lovely crochet rug you'd picked up at the Church Christmas Bazaar made a fine coochie-place for her and she seemed to be very proprietorial once she was strapped into her travel harness and sitting up ready to go.

I remember looking into Rocinante on the morning of your departure and I couldn't help but smile – it had something of the feeling of a person going on a safari or a pilgrimage. You had your atlases, guides to heritage sites, a very impressive camera (I did go and buy exactly the same model only in silver and it is as stunning as you said!), your bed with your spare sleeping bag, your cool box and a huge tool box full of paints and brushes, pastels and pencils. I didn't want you to go because I knew how much I would miss you, but at the same time I was longing to go with you – and if I couldn't go then I couldn't wait to hear news of your travels. Of course at the time I thought it was rather odd that you had purchased a pay as you go phone – and left your ordinary one with me for safe keeping. Now, of course, all is revealed, it was a sensible move.

The inside of the van looked the perfect haven and I recall us playing a sort of a game where I would shout out something I thought you had forgotten to pack and you would have a good rummage through and pull out the object for me to scrutinise!

All too soon it was time for you to go. By then I felt so proud – like the Queen launching a liner. D'you remember I gave you a silly present of some recycled material I had made up on the machine to make bunting. I thought on fine days you could put it round Rocinante. Little did I realise that the last thing you wanted was to draw attention to yourself! I gave you my copy of Pevsner's "Churches" and I was delighted that did come in handy!

As I'm writing Dear Babs, Bella is lying on my feet. It's almost as though she knows I am writing to you. If she wasn't snoring I am sure she would send a big lick and a long tail wag.

I am proud to know you and astonished at your tenacity and vision. Be of good cheer my dear friend. Your present ordeal will not be forever.

With love,
Geraldine   x

4, The Birches,
Brayston,
BY1 4DC.
3rd March

Mr I. Fletcher,
The Manager,
Worth It,
Worth It Retail Park,
Brayston,
BY2 7AR

Dear Mr Fletcher,

    I am writing to ask you to reconsider your store's policy about the way it packages the items that you sell. A lot of packaging is unnecessary and contributes to the rubbish which is not recycled, but makes up bigger and bigger landfill sites. This is a terrible waste and is contributing to the slow destruction of our planet with its limited resources.

    I would like you to respond as to why it is that so much of what you sell is packaged in the current way. I do not think it is enough to say that customers like it this way. You are a powerful business with aggressive buying power. You are well placed, with about a third of the people in this country regularly shopping at one of your stores, to help re-educate and inform people. I think your current policy is short-sighted and destructive. I would like to know what Worth It is going to do to improve its packaging policies.

I look forward to hearing from you. As you have billions of pounds in profit, I am assuming you can afford to send me a reply so I have not enclosed a stamped addressed envelope.

Yours sincerely,

Barbara Drapper

Barbara Drapper SRN (Mrs)

NOW YOU HAVE GONE

By Barbara Drapper

Now you're gone
I sit, looking out of the window
The world does not go on.
With you not there,
I am the ghost that haunts
A thousand places in despair.
Without your smile,
I seek out comfort
And linger for a while.
The house is dead
And I am left alone
With my new friend,
Dread.

EDITED TRANSCRIPT OF PSYCHOTHERAPY SESSION TWO

Name: Barbara Drapper
Hospital Number: 9365286673
DOB: 23.03.44

Consultant: Dr Ishmael Maharinjiti

Psychotherapist: Jessie Arkwright

Extracts from Session Two

...

Jessie: You were very close to Jenny?

Babs: Jenny, my daughter, had a real favourite saying: "It's a sign."

Jessie: I think I've heard you use it too.

Babs: ...I think you're right, I have sort of adopted it in recent years even if it is, was, a bit of a bad family joke. When one of the grandkids was picked for the school football team; when I won that £10 on the Lottery the first time I ever played, we all said – "It's a sign!" I suppose it's a way, just for that split second, of bringing Jen back into the room with us again.

...Jen was absolutely convinced that everything happened for a reason even if we couldn't immediately sort out what it was. I wish I shared her confidence. It's the randomness of it all that ... well it's just random isn't it?

Jessie: The randomness?

Babs: Well I certainly felt like that when Jen was diagnosed with her breast cancer. I loved my daughter. We were friends, you know, in a way at least, not just mother and child. We both knew the writing was on the wall. She'd followed in my footsteps as things turned out even though I'd done my level best to put her off. Nursing by the time she trained wasn't what it had been. It sounds odd, I know, but I felt she could do better for herself – aim higher. You know, she was always her own person even as a little girl. She was as stubborn as an ox – even over silly things like which dress to buy her Barbie doll – never any compromises for our Jen. She went on to do very well for herself, thank you very much.

Jessie: You must have been pleased for her.

Babs: Nursing has changed from my day. The intentions are well meant with Patients' Rights Charter this and consultations and care pathways that, but the job is much more about budgets and targets than the Service would like most of the general public to know. We've forgotten what care is. Too busy trying out the latest techniques; massaging MRSA figures and saving money on the straightforward things. Much more glamorous to pay for interventions which give people little quality of life in reality, just delay the inevitable really and give a few surgeons someone to practise on in the meantime.

Funnily enough once Jen qualified, I always thought she would follow me and become a practice nurse. She'd have enjoyed the variety. She was always a good listener – and she had a light touch – never let you get too down in the dumps. She'd have expected her patients to snap out of it.

Jessie: Jen was very determined.

Babs: Her Dad said she'd been watching too many medical dramas on telly when she told us she was doing the specialist training to become a theatre nurse. Every time she appeared at home, he'd start whistling the theme tune from one of those Accident and Emergency shows. She'd throw a cushion at him! He'd chuckle. He wasn't a great one for telling her how proud he was of her, but he was chuffed to bits with all she'd achieved.

Jessie: You had high hopes for Jen?

Babs: I'd had an urge for Jen to train as a teacher or maybe do something scientific. She was happy though. I hope she was anyway. Her boss said how much she had been liked and respected; how much he missed her as a friend when we were talking after her funeral. I was touched. None of us can ask more than that.

Jessie: Her diagnosis must have been quite a shock?

Babs: When Jenny found her lump she was 31. It felt unreal. The family thought it was somehow worse for her because she was a nurse, but I think it was easier. I've seen hundreds of patients over the years with different cancers. We knew if it was malignant her age would count against her. It turned out to be a virulent form. I suppose we were no different from everyone else. We wanted to make sense of what was happening to us; to Jen. It's very different when it's one of your own.

Jessie: It's different when it's your own.

Babs: We were struggling. Cancer is a hell of a shock at the best of times but we hadn't been a family with a particularly strong history of oestrogen-based cancers. A distant cousin with cancer of the uterus twenty years ago was about it. We all tend to get old

	disgracefully, have strokes and cardio-vascular problems. It was a bolt from the blue.
Jessie:	How did it make you feel?
Babs:	No surprise then that the spread was rapid. At the time you're so caught up in waiting for the next set of test results, offering an ear; making sure there's food on the table and clean clothes in the drawers, not to mention going to work, that time seemed to either race ahead or stand stock still. We were either holding our breath or rushing to get everything done.
Jessie:	How did Jen react?
Babs:	Jen was upbeat. Sometimes I wanted to hit her.
Jessie:	You were feeling–?
Babs:	She wanted us to get on with life and most of the time I could. Sometimes I wanted to feel sorry for myself though. It was all a sign of course. A sign to get on with life. Seize the day.
Jessic:	How did your daughter cope?
Babs:	Jen coped by reading. She devoured everything and anything. *PeopleDirect,* for the support, academic stuff, alternative therapies. She expected me to be up to speed, naturally. She found websites in California trialling some cactus roots for the treatment of breast cancer; then some retired GP in Newcastle who had set herself up as an alternative health practitioner. She cured 'no-hopers' and as we got nearer the end, Jen felt she needed to believe in this woman and gave all her treatments a go. I've never seen so much orange juice drunk in a day. She was trying to use an exercise bike when she could barely walk. Wasn't easy to watch. In reality this so called doctor wasn't doing much more than colonic irrigation and encouraging an organic diet. Jen couldn't really eat

by then. The treatments didn't seem to be doing any harm. It kept Jen focused. It kept her body as clear as possible of all the usual toxins we carry around inside and flooded it with free radicals. That's the key, you see, recognising all the rubbish we force feed our bodies. We expect a machine designed for scavenging and grazing to make use of this additional rubbish we stuff inside ourselves. It's madness.

Jessie: How did you feel about Jen trying the alternative treatments?

Babs: Jen tried all the conventional stuff. The chemo' weakened her beyond belief. The cancer didn't respond – so we visited the local cancer help centre. We learnt to relax; visualise; loads about positive thinking and keeping healthy – stuff you churn out all the time as a nurse – well as a practice nurse. It kept us all busy frankly. I think that was for the best. Then she knew. Jen stopped living in the present. She started living our future. It was her way of getting through the fact that it wasn't going to be hers I suppose. She started planning.

Jessie: Living for now?

Babs: I was devastated for her, but I couldn't see what more I could do. She wanted me to go with her flow. You can mid-wife death just like you do birth.

Jessie: It must have been hard.

Babs: Jen was frantic. She'd found this woman in Bridelcombe Darcett who was seriously into making alternative coffins – out of cardboard. She ordered one that looked a bit like a papier-mâché cocoon and we all got together one Saturday and helped decorate it. I couldn't get enthusiastic about the blessed thing, but the kids and Alan seemed to think it was fun, painting and glueing for several days to get it all done. They even put some fanfare thing on the stereo and had it all covered up in the lounge for a special unveiling ceremony for us all to admire the finished product. I'm glad they didn't decide to go with Jen's original plan which was that the wider family would see it first on the day of the funeral, I think my sister would have had an apoplectic fit. For anyone else I would have thought it fitting somehow. It was very personal and beautiful in its way. Photos of the family and big flowers painted by Natalie; Matthew's favourite cartoon superhero carefully drawn by him with a big speech bubble saying "To eternity and beyond". It was very Jen. Funny, I'd not thought before, but I suppose I was a bit disappointed. I wanted something normal; conventional for Jen, like we'd done for Derek. The personalised bit of Jen's death for me was that it was my daughter doing the dying. I think I wanted her death to somehow be contained. Conventional ways keep things looking normal. Just like everyone's sadness and pain. There was nothing special or different about our hurt – except it was us doing the hurting.

Jessie: You felt ripped apart.

Babs: Jen went to so much trouble to make her death easier for us. I don't think she realised, bless her, she couldn't control that part. We were all given memory boxes which were to be opened after her death. Alan and I had the job of distributing these to immediate family. There were CDs of photos and messages, and a present for each of the kids to open and another for when they were 18 and if they get married. Loads of stuff. It was almost too thoughtful. I looked in mine a week after the funeral. I wasn't ready. I suppose it will be in store now.

Jessie: How do you feel about Jen's death now?

Babs: Now, looking back I would rather have had the memories of time together. But we all meant well. Those last weeks were all rushing to buy CDs and hurrying out with lists of gifts to get. Maybe she just wanted to keep Alan and me busy. I don't know. He seemed to be up half the night burning photos on to CDs. Every now and then we'd slip in and spend time with her and then get back to our jobs.

Jessie: You feel you missed out on something?

Babs: We had a fit of the giggles one night at about three in the morning. We couldn't stop. I hadn't laughed so much in years. Alan had been in their box room trying to get yet another lot of poems and photos onto disc for Jen's Uncle Rob's Memory Box. I had been in the lounge at the coffee table trying to wrap more special presents in rainbow coloured paper. We'd met in the hall outside their bedroom door. We'd needed a break – and had had the same idea – we'd go and sit with Jen. Alan was just about to open the door for me when I said to him. Oh, I can't recall the exact words – but something like – "I wonder if the elves feel like this in Lapland". I meant exhausted. Well, that did it. We were off. We must have made so much noise that we woke Jen up – "What are you laughing at?" she said.

"You," we said and she was back off to sleep in a second.

Jessie: How do you feel about Jen now, Babs?

Babs: I want her back. I miss having her to worry about and fuss over. I expect it's always the way. I often wonder if it's different when you have more than one child. Jen died a year last Christmas. She was truly worn out, poor love. She needed to be shot of that body. It was doing her no good at all.

She wanted to be buried in a Woodland Burial Site. We did as we were told. Not with her Dad and where I'm to go.

We go back.

Well, they do now. We've added bulbs – spring flowers. Always was her favourite time of the year. Spring Hope she'd call it.

The children don't go so much now, I believe, not since Alan's married Alison and the baby's on the way. They've moved anyway to be nearer to Alison's new job. He wants them to have a new life. Be a proper family; it's their chance to move on. He says I've seen to that.

Jessie: How do you feel about that?

Babs: It does feel harsh, yes, but they need to make their own sense of what has happened to them…

Canalside Cottage,
Chandler's Lane,
Wynleigh,
Brayston BY3 2PG

My Dear Babs,

What a lovely surprise your last letter was! Despite your present difficulties you sound remarkably positive. I am terribly sorry to read that the psychiatric assessment feels so intrusive and "dire". It is never easy to open oneself up to strangers especially when, as you say, you're not entirely sure what it is they are looking for.

For what it's worth, I would be inclined to trust them. However sceptical you may be of mental health provision because of your professional role, it may be a little easier if you can see these people as people – not as the enemy who are trying to get you to incriminate yourself. I think I can empathise with your feeling that you are a political prisoner with a small 'p'. Even so, these people are not interrogators; they are professionally qualified to assess what support you need. You would be super human if you didn't need some support at some level after all you have been through. I do not, for one minute, believe that they think you are mad. Not only is that probably non-pc these days – but quite clearly there is insurmountable evidence to the contrary! I would encourage you not to second guess them – and try – after all these months of not being able to be fully yourself – to get back to the real Babs; the one I know who is full of compassion and generosity of spirit. Right, you'll be relieved to hear that is my nag over and done with.

I was looking out paper etc... for recycling the other day and found my box of your postcards. To be honest with you, I had a little cry because I am and I do miss you hugely. I particularly value the ones you painted. You were quite wrong when you said your Salisbury Cathedral watercolour had a "too big and wonky" spire. I had a good look at it again this morning and I think you have caught the proportions perfectly – it is a huge spire, let's face it!

I found a card you had written to me from Bella too which made me laugh just as it did at the time! How you managed to be so creative and so thoughtful with all that you were doing and carrying emotionally I cannot begin to fathom.

I was contacted the other day by the police and I have been over to collect some things that were in Rocinante. She's still impounded of course. I have stored them in my spare room rather than take them back to your bungalow. I hope this is alright with you. I went over and aired the bungalow yesterday. I have put the heating a little higher as we are in a cold snap, but I will be over to turn it down as soon as the milder weather returns. The bungalow is such a calm and peaceful place. I have asked Steve who has been helping me out with my own garden to put some sessions in on yours – we'll call it an un-birthday gift! We need to have it spick and span when you return!

In haste to catch the post –

Your friend, as ever,

Geraldine   x

[Kept in Barbara's wallet with a photograph of Jen, Alan, Natalie and Matthew]

My Grandma

Thank you Grandma for all that you do,
for mum and dad and Matt and me.
You take us to the park, and sing,
and play and make me feel happy.
When I am down and fed up with life,
you find the words to help me see
That everything will be all right,
when I have had a cup of tea.
I love your puddings and your pies.
I love the way you cross your eyes.
I love the woolly scarf you knit,
I love the way you walk and sit.
I love it when we play games
And give the clouds funny names.
I love the rabbit ear cakes you bake
And I love the love you give and do not take.

To Grandma

Love from

Natalie Age 11   X X X X X

HMP Starling

14th February

Dear Natalie,

I was getting together the papers to go with my letter to you and I couldn't help sitting down and reading them. I don't think I bothered to read them properly when I first got them. They have to give you copies of just about everything, it's your human right - but you do get bogged down.

It's funny how fast things can change in life. One minute you think you know what you're about and you can see a way through and the next you are struggling to make sense of all that's happening.

Reading through what I said to the psychotherapist, Jessica Arkwright, I wanted to be sure that you knew just how important you and Matthew are to me. I haven't included the whole transcripts as they are a bit long and a lot of what I said about you and Matthew was muddled in with stuff about your mum and dad. Sometimes I felt angry your mum had died and hurt that your dad wasn't keen on me seeing you.

I do remember showing her your poem which I had asked if I could keep with me when I handed in my wallet. We both agreed that you had a gift with words and I told her how much you meant to me.

What I have never done is to tell you, in so many words, to your face, how much I love you and how much I value you as a person. You can say I am biased, but I think you are very intelligent, caring, funny, sensitive and kind. When I think about you I see your smile and picture you sitting at your dressing table brushing your hair.

When I think of Matthew, he's drawing or hitting those buttons on his console and shooting ships in space. I remember a serious boy, gentle, concerned and a very loving companion. I can still probably tell at least one Railway Station story from memory thanks to Matt.

Thank you both for giving me these things.

Your loving

Grandma Babs

xxxx

> Canalside Cottage,
> Chandler's Lane,
> Wynleigh,
> Brayston BY3 2PG

My Dear Babs,

I can't begin to tell you how saddened I was by your last letter. Can it really be true that after all you have been through you now have to face cancer on top of everything else? You sound so hopeless as though there is nothing to be done – but surely there must be SOMETHING. Modern science offers so many possibilities – are you sure you have explored all your options?

I do understand, and I am so sorry if my tone belies this, that you feel you have had enough, but I do beg you to consider that this may be a sign of your weariness at the hand life has dealt you, rather than a desire not to survive. I know you to be a woman with an iron will. If you set your heart on something it will happen. I urge you to consider reclaiming your life rather than letting it slip away from you.

I can quite understand you not factoring an old crony like me into your equations, but I am surprised you are placing so little weight on your grandchildren's happiness. Yes, I know Alan has a very poor opinion of you these days and has forbidden contact with the children, but do reflect on the fact that they are growing, they will not always be under his jurisdiction, and from what you have told me about them I would be astounded if they didn't want to seek you out as young adults.

Think too of all you have done. However cowardly custard I am about some of what you did, there's no two ways about it, you have challenged a nation's understanding of what healthy is and what is genuinely sustainable. Of course, you know that I believe the final campaign went too far, but I can only gaze on with awe that you had the vision to do it. You were utterly single-minded; things had to change in order to save lives. I know you feel the sentencing was harsh and that an unnecessary example was made of you. I know your time in prison is hard and wearing. I also know that the Babs I love as a sister would not be true to herself if she just gave up the ghost and said, "Right, that's it, I'm not striving anymore". You are the person who taught me the meaning of standing up for what you believe in. I would be a fool if I didn't persuade you at this horrendously trying time to continue with the task you feel called to undertake – for the sake of others if you cannot make it for your own sake.

God bless you.

I am praying for you – as is my church.

With much love,

Geraldine   x

LONG GONE

I am lost, alone and a long way from home;
I think of you each day and wish that I could say,
How much I love you.
But all I see is darkness, there's no longing just an emptiness,
I am dumb and numb and low.
I watch the people move around me
Like actors on the TV and I wonder why they bother with me and won't
Leave me on my own.
I see their smiling faces turn to well-meaning grimaces
As they try to make some sense of my
Ever present woes.
I just want to turn my head away,
And sleep myself to death TODAY
And pray that this would all just go away
And I was all alone.   BD

EDITED TRANSCRIPT OF PSYCHOTHERAPY SESSION THREE

Name: Barbara Drapper
Hospital Number: 9365286673
DOB: 23.03.44

Consultant: Dr Ishmael Maharinjiti

Psychotherapist: Jessie Arkwright

Extracts from Session Three

Jessie: How do you feel about the planning now?

Babs: Looking back all the planning was an absolute saving grace. I don't know what I would have done during those first few months after Jenny's death without it.

...

I've seen many patients over the years as they get close to death and I reckoned I'd spot the signs when it was Jen's time. Maybe she double-bluffed me. I wouldn't put it past her. Maybe she was trying to protect me right to the end. When it came, it was on a better than average day. She'd seemed a bit stronger. Maybe when push came to shove I just couldn't bear to face the fact that my own flesh and blood was dying before my eyes. I don't know. Whatever, I was sure we had days if not weeks left. Maybe she relaxed and her heart just gave out. Deep down I think she knew. Maybe she was seizing her day – when the time just ran out.

Jessie: You sound cheated by Jen's death?

Babs: I was determined to retire on the dot of turning 60. I'd given pretty much all my working life to the NHS and I was needed by my child. I ended up staying on of course, helping the new girl out part-time. I regret that. I wanted more than anything in the world to be there for Jen. The tables were turned, yes. The odd times I had given it some thought I'd always imagined she would one day be looking after me.

Jessie: And Jen had died and left you.

Babs: I gave up work at the end of November. She died the day after Boxing Day. I replay those last days again and again. I missed something. Maybe she didn't tell me what she was telling the Macmillan nurse. He was a nice lad, Jamie Crocker. None of the professionals seemed surprised. The Macmillan had seen it coming. Maybe my eyes were blinkered. Too much wishful thinking. All that professional nurse stuff flew out of the window. It was my baby Jenny lying there dead.

Jessie: How did you feel Babs?

Babs: I laid her out myself. I'd brought her into the world. I felt it was the very least I could do. I couldn't do that for Derek and I was sorry.

Jessie: You were sorry.

Babs: We got the coffin from the garage, so there wasn't much the funeral chaps needed to do. Jen had chosen a firm on the High Street with a lady director. I knew the foreman. Former patient. Lovely, old-fashioned chap. Used to work for the Co-op. Poached by better wages and working conditions at the independent funeral firm down the road, he'd said. I think he must have arranged to be on when Jen's funeral happened. It was nice to see his friendly face casting an eye over everything.

Jessie: How was the funeral for you?

Babs: The morning after the funeral was the most difficult, there's no two ways about it. It was a misery of a day. It didn't bother to get light. Natalie and Matthew, Jen's little ones (how they'd hate me for saying that now – Natalie is 14 and Matthew is 10) had gone into school that day for the first time since their mum's death. Alan, my son-in-law had seen them in. He texted to say they were OK. I'd stayed over off and on during the weeks before Jen's death and then stayed the whole time up to the funeral. I was doing the practical stuff really, making sure there was a warm meal at night even if we didn't feel much like eating – keeping house I suppose. Alan needed some space – so the kids and I would go to the pictures or the park or swimming. Normal stuff really.

...

I'd got it in mind that if Alan and the children were all right with it, I would go back home on the night of the funeral. Alan was fine and very appreciative, I thought, of my being about. I think he probably meant what he said. He could have managed perfectly well without me of course. Probably would have made life a lot simpler for him in reality, so I said how grateful I had been that he had let me be around. We parted on good terms and anyway, I was going back that next night with a special treat, fish and chip supper, because it was first day back at work and school and all.

Jessie: How did you feel about leaving Alan and your grandchildren?

Babs: I felt they were ready to see me go. I needed to see my own four walls. Jen would have said I needed 'a duvet day'. I have to say that was the last thing I

	wanted. Every bone in my body was made of lead – my head was free-ranging.
Jessie:	You couldn't think?
Babs:	Once the caterers had cleared away, I ran the Hoover through the lounge and set off for home. Natalie texted me at her bedtime to let me know that all was well. I planned to be back at theirs in time to welcome Matthew home from school next day. Coming home to an empty house wasn't good for the lad.

...

I sat at my kitchen table that first morning. I just could not move. Somehow I got myself a cup of coffee, hoping, I suppose, that it might pep me up, but when I came to it, it was cold. I don't know what I was thinking about. I just felt in a bit of a daze. I couldn't get my mind into gear. I heard the mail drop through the letter box. I'd have usually been on to that as I quite like getting post. I knew how I felt was to be expected. I didn't feel ill. I didn't feel anything. The radio was burbling away in the background. I couldn't remember switching it on but I knew I must have. I don't know how long I was sitting there, but I didn't shift until the end of *World at Midday*.

...

FIT FOR NOTHING

What can I say,
I am ashamed to be me
To have done what I have done
To breathe the same air
As people who are good and fair.
I am a wretched, stupid woman
With wickedness in her heart,
And a perverted sense of what is right,
A fool, a thief, a nonsense of a woman
Who deserves to have no family and no friends.
Who should be shut away as if time never ends.
I am worthy of no more favours
No more support
No more care
No more hope
I deserve to die
To be treated as I dared treat other people.
I am worse than words can tell.

4, The Birches,
Brayston,
BY1 4DC.

15th March

Mr I. Fletcher,
The Manager,
Worth It,
Worth It Retail Park,
Brayston,
BY2 7AR

Dear Mr Fletcher,

I wrote to you on 3rd March asking you to reply and explain to me how Worth It stores are going to improve their packaging so that there is less waste just being buried in landfill.

You have not had the courtesy to reply, which I find disturbing and irresponsible. You are the biggest supermarket chain in this country. This huge stake in our shopping does not come without some responsibilities. I think it is important that you are accountable to the people who choose to shop at your shops.

I have enclosed a stamped addressed envelope and anticipate a reply at your earliest convenience.

Yours sincerely,

Barbara Drapper

Barbara Drapper SRN (Mrs)

HMP Starling

20th February

Dear Natalie,

I haven't been at all well over the last couple of days. I've had trouble keeping food down which is a nuisance!

I don't want you thinking that caring for you was anything other than a joy and a pleasure. I loved it.

Looking back I think I felt so down because everything just piled in on top of me. I couldn't see the wood for the trees. I felt as though I had left my feelings in the ice box. They have taken forever to begin to thaw out. I've read about this sort of thing, but never really experienced it myself.

When Grandad Derek died it was a terrible shock but somehow I couldn't be sad for too long. He had thoroughly enjoyed life and he would have hated some long illness. He always said if he couldn't go in his sleep he would like to have a heart attack whilst watching a number 7 car win at the races. At least it was quick and he suffered no pain. It's funny the things I can be thankful for, even pleased about now.

I love the silly little things we shared together Natalie. Making jam tarts, French knitting, sorting out the kitchen cupboards. You trying to teach me the abbreviations when texting! PeopleDirect - which I could never remember my password for! Your laughter was infectious.

I think I must have been tired and depressed for quite a while. More exhausted than I ever thought possible - it was my body's way of giving me some time to sort myself out inside. Time to remember what really matters in life.

Life is for living Natalie - and enjoying.

Make sure you find plenty of things you love doing.

Life's very short when you are looking back.

I was very, very happy to be your Grandma and Matthew's. I know it wasn't the same as mum being there - but

I was glad I had the chance to be around and learn so much from both of you (and I don't just mean how to text!)

LOTS of love or lol

Your Grandma Babs.

Canalside Cottage,
Chandler's Lane,
Wynleigh,
Brayston BY3 2PG

My Dear Babs,

I have read your letter over and over again. Where do I begin, my dear friend? I suppose I must commence by putting your mind at rest. Yes, I will help with such preparations and other things you feel you will need as you prepare to die and after you are dead. I was very upset and unsettled by your letter and so I took the liberty of taking it to our Rector, Grace. She has helped me to see how best I can support you with compassion and acceptance. I do believe this is not the only way or the best way forward. I cannot reiterate this enough, but as Grace says, "This is your decision and no amount of haranguing her will help". So you see I am learning my lesson.

Getting you a coffin and such I would rather do after you have died if you don't mind. If you have strong feeling about type and so forth, I think you will have to give me further instructions. At this point my biggest fear is that I get something wrong. As far as other matters go, now you are waiting for a release date I am hopeful we will be able to talk more freely and openly before the Inevitable Event.

Fighting for you and with you,

Your friend,

Geraldine   x

CRACKING THE CODE

By Barbara Drapper

Your actions are masked
With forced sleight-of-hand
And clever misdirection
As you recite familiar words –
'We are only giving people what they want, cheap food'.
I can crack the code.
With a well-practised skill
You steal my family,
You shuffle the cards of my expectations
And deal your commitment
To destroy the very people who keep you working.
I can crack the code.
With unbelievable timing you show
The card I would never have chosen.
Your slimy businessman charm
Is mocking and cruel.
I'm glad I don't believe you mean it.
I can crack your code.
I can cut your marked deck,
Rearrange the foods like suits on a rail,
But you know the lay of the cards,
And you think you're the winner,
You'll try and take us all.
For fools.
But I will break your chain.
As if by magic you appear
To sell us the dream none of us can own.
As if we asked you for it
You feed us rubbish and rob us of our money
You destroy our planet and tell us this is what we want.
And we believe you.
But I will break your chain.
I can crack your code.

EDITED TRANSCRIPT OF PSYCHOTHERAPY SESSION FOUR

Name: Barbara Drapper
Hospital Number: 9365286673
DOB: 23.03.44

Consultant: Dr Ishmael Maharinjiti

Psychotherapist: Jessie Arkwright

Extracts from Session Six

...

Jessie: I want to go back over the last session a little bit ... How were you feeling after your daughter died?

Babs: I still felt like a zombie when I was round with the grandchildren. They were full of energy, especially Matt, and I felt empty. Natalie was no sooner in the door than she was texting ninety to the dozen. Matt needed to be around me. Wanted to keep me close. I listened to him read. It was soothing. Familiar. Like old times.

Jessie: The familiar helped?

Babs: There was already talk of a live-in Nanny. Alan showed me the advert. I felt I should make tracks. They needed time to regroup; to learn how to be a family without Jen's help and my interference. I knew that, but I felt nothing.

...

Jessie: How did you feel inside, Babs?

Babs: Well, it was like I was watching not very convincing actors trying to work their way through a really badly written episode of a soap.

Jessie: You felt disassociative or disconnected?

Babs: I could not sleep. Up until then sleep had always been a bit of a defence mechanism. I'd have a sleep if I had a headache. Have an afternoon nap in the chair if I felt a bit pooped. I wasn't one of life's great worriers or analysers. What happens, happens and you just have to get on with it.

Jessie: Do you still feel that's true for you?

Babs: Then there was that night I could not sleep. I didn't feel anxious, at least I don't think I did. Hard to tell thinking back. I just could not sleep. Bit ironic really. I had dished out advice often enough at the surgery to patients with sleeping difficulties, now I had to follow my own *Golden Rules*. It's given a fancy name these days – sleep hygiene. Reminds me of dental floss. It's just common sense really.

Jessie: Common sense?

Babs: Except I forgot the part about how sleep should refresh you.

I concentrated on the rituals. There was no point in waiting until I was sleepy. I felt wide awake at night and exhausted all day.

Jessie: Did you try and sleep during the day at all?

Babs: Yes, I'd cat nap, but not so much that I thought it would interfere with night-time. I'd have the warm bath and milky drink. I tried one of the relaxation tapes I'd bought for Jen, but the memories. Hopeless. Something that had to be endured. I knew whatever I tried wouldn't work.

Jessie: What were your rituals?

Babs: Watch the *Ten O'clock News*. Lock up. Collect a glass of water. Loo. Quick wash. Clean teeth. Bed. No sleep.

Jessie: Difficult.

Babs: I didn't used to read in bed. I was one of those who would flop into bed exhausted after a busy day and be sound asleep in seconds.

Sometimes my mind would get the better of me. Usually some problem about work, but nine times out of ten I was off before I had decided what I should have said to Brenda or someone else who'd irritated me that day.

Jessie: What was so difficult about Brenda?

Babs: Oh don't ask, she was the receptionist from hell.

Jessie: So what changed?

Babs: When Derek was alive, I was terrible. He only had to start to tell me about his plans for pricking out in the greenhouse and I was out like a light.

Jessie: Then after Jen's death sleeping became –

Babs: That night all that changed; well, I just lay there, didn't I? I tossed. I turned. I rearranged the pillows. I took a pillow away. Counted sheep. Even dressed them up in fancy costumes and then made them jump the gate. Radio on. Radio off. Went out on the landing and chose one of those bodice ripper novels I bought in the '90s. The words just danced. I wasn't interested. Couldn't have cared less who fancied who.

I got to sleep eventually. Felt like five minutes.

Jessie: What was the daytime like?

Babs: No, there was nothing special about that next day except I did start to feel uneasy in the evening. I didn't want to go to bed. Right. No bed. Chose not to make a thing of it. Decided I would stay up and watch the late film. Pretty gruesome as it turned out. I don't have a stomach for violence. Channel hopped. No joy. Watching kids waiting for paternity results and screaming at each other didn't help. I was restless. I didn't realise that's what it was. Didn't know what to do with myself. I kept telling myself not to be such a lazy missy and get off my backside and do something constructive. It wasn't me who had died. The house needed a clean for starters. The ironing wasn't going to do itself. I don't know why but for once in my life I just groaned at the thought of it all. I couldn't sleep, but I didn't want to do anything either.

Jessie: How did this make you feel?

Babs: I was a bit on edge, looking back. I think I realised that. I took my blood pressure. Surprise, surprise a little inflated. I'd never been a great one for going out at night. We did ballroom for a bit when we were younger. Mostly for the social life rather than the dancing. It was good fun and we made some nice friends. Now and again I did the odd evening class. Nothing too fancy. I wanted something to relax with after a busy day. I discovered a real treasure that way. I found out that I loved art. I wasn't that bothered about how the picture looked at the end. I loved the messing about with the paint, the mixing; the feel of chalk. I suppose it was like being back at school. Some of the class were very competitive and did paintings for exhibitions. Always sounding off about winning this or that prize. One chap used to sell stuff. But the corner I usually sat in had a group of us ladies who were there because we liked to be there. Learnt a bit about our families. We were supportive of each other's efforts, such as they were.

Jessie: It sounds as though painting became very important to you.

Babs: I learnt how to escape into another world.

Jessie: So you painted to escape?

Babs: Funniest of things really. My sister Doreen gave me a set of acrylic paints, a pad and some scrapbook making materials one Christmas. Well, I thought she was being funny, but I tried to be generous, you know, as I actually unwrapped it all. Doreen's into her leisure pursuits – and her dogs. Derek always said that was half her trouble – she had far too much time on her hands. There may have been some truth in that. He never took to Doreen. I think he was always a bit jealous. Saw her as a bit of a rival as far as my attention was concerned. He got on well enough with Doreen's Rob though. Anyhow, when I opened this present my first thoughts were far from charitable. I thought she was harking back to when we were children. Everyone always said she was the talented and artistic one. I was the plodder with no imagination. Doreen smelt a rat, saw I wasn't very enthusiastic about her present.

Jessie: You felt disappointed?

Babs: We were in the kitchen preparing lunch. She asked me if everything was all right. I prattled on for a bit about this and that. I don't drink much, so it was probably the sherry talking, but I launched into this stuff about her choice of present for her 'only sister'.

Jessie: It sounds as though it was unusual for you to be so forthright in those days?

Babs: The weird bit was that her recollection was totally different from mine. She was sure that I was the one who had always been praised for beautiful art work. She thought she was the one who was hopeless. She thought she'd been doing me a favour. She hoped I'd get in touch with my inner child.

Jessie: How did that make you feel?

Babs: She'd started a Christian counselling course at her local church. She'd been reflecting on her family relationships that particular term. She reminded me of the big painting I'd done one summer. I had completely forgotten.

I do remember it had felt a really long, boring summer holiday. We had stayed home for the whole time. Money worries I shouldn't wonder. We'd taken a break earlier in the year in Blackpool; our usual hotel near the pier on South Shore. It seemed like a lifetime ago. I bored easily in those days. Probably one crush done and dusted and not yet found the next object of my desire. I was a fickle girl. Mother suggested that I got my old paints out. I gave her quite a lecture about babyish things and said I wanted to do proper things with my time and that a shortage of money meant I couldn't enjoy myself. She bit her tongue, I'm sure. My friend had got a job just for Saturdays in Woolworth's and I was as jealous as hell. Not the job so much as the money. Her clothes mainly.

Jessie: The summer was long and boring?

Babs: Boredom must have really set in. I searched. Requisitioned the kitchen table and set up the paints on it with a chipped cup with pink flowers and a gold line around the lip for my water. I'd never attempted a painting before which I went back to again and again. At school I'd dash stuff off in a lesson. Move on. Mostly film stars and boys. I quite liked copying faces and making them quite cartoon-like.

I spent hours on this painting. It became an almost everyday thing. Getting the newspaper out and spreading it over the wooden table Mother had inherited from Uncle Jack. Finding my cup in the cupboard which mother had always managed to put to the back so we didn't use a chipped cup because of the germs, but still sure it would come in useful one day. Filling from the cold water tap, just enough, not too much. Just so far. Getting my painting hankie ready and sitting in my chair. Check the table. Race upstairs and pull the painting out from under the bed where I'd left it to dry the day before – and where no one would think to look.

Jessie: Were you worried about someone looking, Babs?

Babs: I had a pact with myself if anyone looked and laughed at it. That was it. I was going to throw it.

Jessie: Throw your work away?

Babs: The painting started out as an ordinary piece of A4. I had plans for a landscape. Comic strip style. Lots of bright colours. I thought I'd have it finished after a couple of hours. But I wasn't satisfied with the result. It looked like a much younger child's work. Fairytale garden with a house and a big tree. For some reason I didn't just screw it up and bin it. I put it under my divan.

Jessie: Do you have a sense of why you kept it?

Babs: I was eating *Corn Flakes* next morning. Always a bone of contention in our house because Doreen and I wanted *Sugar Puffs*. Doreen was probably chattering on about some dish of a lad she'd seen.

Jessie: Seen?

Babs: Yes, seen. Chance as not. She spent most of that summer working down at the local ice rink. She was quite shy for all her chatter. I was sitting there half listening when I had an idea for the painting. I'd more or less decided in the bath that I was going to throw it as soon as I could find a moment to get downstairs and out to the dustbin without anyone seeing it. I think mother was a little suspicious that something was up when I actually offered to help clear the breakfast things away. She looked relieved when she saw the newspaper and paints coming out.

Jessie: How did you get along with your mother?

Babs: She did her best, Mother. She even tried to make some encouraging noises when I plucked up the courage to show her the work in progress. She said she was looking forward to seeing my next one. I tore off three sheets and placed them with the painting. I can remember like it was yesterday. It didn't sit right. It pushed the now blurry, smudgy house to one side, to the other, then slightly off centre. Now I know about hot spots in a composition – the points on the canvas that your eye is drawn to – I would know where to place the house. Then it was all instinctive. Experimental. New.

Took me a while to realise that what I really needed were eight sheets with the smudge house in the centre. I think deep down I must have rather rated the smudge house once it had dried. I stole my Dad's brown parcel tape from the lounge bureau and started sticking the sheets together.

Jessie: Did you steal much as a child?

Babs: Then came the difficult part. Mother was busy hanging the washing out in the garden. Never a good moment to ask a favour. I made her a cuppa. We sat in the old deckchair and the aluminium sun chair on the bald patch in the lawn and she sipped her tea and I scratched a bit at the earth with the toe of my shoe till she told me not to scuff it.

Jessie: Was it an uncomfortable silence between you?

Babs: No, it wasn't an uncomfortable silence. More enjoying the sunshine and the breeze. It was like we just didn't have particular things to say. Though of course I was busting. I had.

Jessie: Was your Mother a good listener?

Babs: I offered to weed the flowerbed by our chairs. It was my favourite. Right by the apple tree and carefully laid out with a row of clumpy lobelia, marigolds, tobacco plants, some straggly lavender and the old rose bushes. Some dandelions were taking root and it hadn't had a good going over since we'd planted it out. Mother rested her head on the deckchair back. Shut her eyes.

Jessie: How did you interpret that, Babs?

Babs: She told me about her Father. For the umpteenth time. Her Father making her double dig the veg' patch and work out on the allotment in all weathers. I bit my lip. I asked if she had any old magazines she didn't need anymore. To use for my paintings. She looked a bit taken a back. She said I could help myself from the bookshelf in the lounge as long as I cleared up properly.

Jessie: Have you a sense of how long you spent on the painting?

Babs: I can't remember how long it took to finish the picture, not all told, but Doreen was right. For ages Mother and Dad had it up on the wall on the upstairs landing. Dad pasted it to a sort of hardboard back. I had forgotten. Probably got taken down when the

Christmas decorations went up. Thrown out years back. So Doreen got me painting again. Derek called it my 'love affair with a paint box'. Her present sat on the sideboard for weeks. I'd thought I might give it to one of the grandchildren, but I knew Doreen would be hurt. Then as the kids were going back to school, the usual circular dropped through the door advertising that year's evening classes at the local schools and college. Derek always had a good look at it to see if there was anything interesting in the gardening line. This particular autumn he spotted a Wednesday evening class in pest control. Well, I put my foot down I can tell you. What with his pub quiz night, darts team, stock car on Saturdays and helping Rob and Doreen out at the kennels at the drop of a hat I was wondering when I was going to get a look in.

Jessie: Were you angry with Derek?

Babs: I suppose I was. But my Derek had an answer for everything – "why don't you take a course too, love," he said, "then we can meet up for a date at the coffee break." I told him – in his dreams, and he said he'd see me behind the bike sheds. Derek spotted there was a needlework course and this painting one.

Jessie: Derek sounds supportive?

Babs: That night when I got so agitated. When I just couldn't settle. Didn't know what to do with myself. Quite suddenly I needed to go out. I remember thinking it was madness. It was after two in the morning. I tell you what though, I think more than anything else I wanted anonymity. Being somewhere I could forget. Forget the last hours of Jen dying and me not knowing. Forget the terrible shock of the policeman at the door telling me Derek had had an accident, when what he really meant was he was dead. Forget.

Jessie: Not being able to forget is very painful.

Babs: It was the pain of watching people suffer. Forget how bewildered, yes, bewildered and lost I was.

Jessie: Do you think this tipped you into planning the campaign with which you are charged?

Babs: I don't want to talk about that right now. I'm sorry. I know you think it might help. Not now. Not yet.

Jessie: So where did you choose to go that night?

Babs: I took the car into the town centre. I wasn't thinking. It took a while before I realised it might not be safe to just park up and wander through the precinct on my own. I doubled back, drove out the way I'd come, past the turning down to the house, on along the dual carriageway and under the flyover. The bright lights of the retail park. I pulled onto the slip road and into *Worth It*'s car park. I never thought I'd see the day I was happy about 24 hour opening.

The store is very different at night. None of the screeching and chatter. It's slower, more meticulous somehow.

Shelves being stacked. Wheelchair users shopping; folk alone. The strugglers in an alien world I called them. I felt at home. No eye contact. No chatter. What was there to talk about? I took one of the smallest trolleys. I can remember saying to myself, this is ridiculous, take a basket, get some milk and go. What do you need a trolley for? I walked aimlessly along the magazine aisle. I picked out a local paper and a *Defender*. I grabbed some glucose drink from the cool cabinet and thought I'd sit in the closed café once I was fed up with exploring the store and read. I felt a little shaky and put that down to blood sugar levels. I should have taken the larger trolley. The man on the till was a help and called for an assistant to carry the boxes and bags out to my car. He even told me that he thought my kit was neat.

Jessie: Did the visit help?

Babs: I wasn't ready to go back to the house. I went back into *Worth It*. I sat with the paper and drink in the semi darkness of the café. I looked at my watch. It was only a little bit after three. I was sure it had to be much later than that.

I watched a few cars come and go. I tried to read the paper. Nothing doing. Couldn't concentrate to save my life. Some part of me just wanted to snap out of it and be back home. I couldn't do it. Go home. I cried. I hadn't cried for ages. Not for months. I cried. Right there in a supermarket. Madness. Came from nowhere.

Jessie: Madness?

Babs: Geraldine's hand was on my shoulder. I looked up and for a second thought I was dreaming and was relieved I'd managed to get to sleep after all. She put down her bags and pulled up a chair. I looked down at her shopping and I had to smile – all the packaging was intact. Geraldine saw me looking and apologised profusely. She couldn't keep it up you see. The store staff had made her feel so ashamed. She'd been frog-marched out one day and the guard wouldn't let her pay.

Jessie: You sounded very pleased she appeared?

Babs: She shopped in the night to avoid any trouble. I thought it might be to avoid me too, but she looked with such kindly eyes at me that I couldn't help myself, I burst into tears again. She said she admired me. She wished she still had the courage to try and put some of the truly important things in society right. I thought that was a really lovely thing to say to someone. I didn't believe her, but it was a really nice thought.

...

MISCHIEF GENE

By Barbara Drapper

In each and every human being
There is a mischief gene,
Which when it is fed and watered
Nurtured and played with,
Grows into a magical thing.
A charming, risky,
Riotous, rebel of an entity,
That will test a human's rationality.
Mischief niggles at the heart of man
She listens hard to the unsettling words
That fill the head and press the heart
Turns commonsense into drifting sand.
Mischief settles on the least expected,
The one thought dismissed as mad speculation.
Mischief takes the thought and weaves a tale
Which when revisited by a humble mind becomes
The one desired thing.
Mischief sets to work
And hand in hand
With the naïve soul
Takes on the world
And tries to transform her woe.

CONFIDENTIAL: NOT TO BE COPIED WITHOUT THE CONSENT OF THE PATIENT	Department of Psychiatry, Terrington House, St. Margaret's Hospital, Wellingbridge WE2 7KG Telephone: 01989 303565 www.show.eng.nhs.uk/nhswellingbridgeshire/

CONFIDENTIAL
PSYCHOLOGICAL MULTIDISCIPLINARY REPORT
30th September

Hospital Number: 9365286673

Consultant:	Dr I. Maharinjiti
SpR:	Dr H. MacAllister
SHO:	Dr V. Goode
Date of Admission:	29th August
Date of Discharge:	30th September
Name:	Barbara Elizabeth Drapper
Address:	4, The Birches, Brayston, BY1 4DC
Telephone:	01723 324321
DOB:	23.03.1944
Marital Status:	Widow
N o K:	Geraldine Hammond, Willow Cottage, Chandler's Lane, Wynleigh, Brayston BY3 2PG. 01723 825001
Religion:	Church of England
Ethnicity:	Caucasian, British.

Demographics:

Barbara is a British Caucasian woman aged 63. She lives alone in a three bed-roomed bungalow in Brayston. She is currently on remand awaiting psychiatric reports and medical tests at HMP Starling.

Mode of Referral:

Barbara was referred to Terrington House following her remand at HMP Starling on 28th August this year. A period of in-patient assessment was provided.

Presenting Issues and History of Presenting Issues:

1. Barbara has been charged with 'Administering poison or noxious things with intent to injure, aggrieve or annoy, contrary to section 24 Offences Against the Person Act 1861'.

2. Barbara is alleged to have undertaken a campaign against the supermarket chain Worth It by placing messages written on rice paper using food colouring inside packets of food. These packets of food were purchased from the store and then returned to the shelf or cold cabinet with the message concealed inside, later the same day. The packaging appeared to be intact to the consumer at the time of their purchase. Barbara is alleged to have tampered with the packaging in order to place the message inside

and then injected some foodstuffs with green food dye to give the impression the food may be inedible. The messages were intended to inform purchasers that the food would damage their health. For example, she is alleged to have written:

"Eat this get cancer die".

3. The police apprehended Barbara Drapper on 17th August and charged her on the advice of the Crown Prosecution Service on 20th August following an incident in which a customer with learning disabilities purchased a packet of *Pie Man* Ready Cooked Cocktail Sausages and ate the whole contents including the rice paper message. The customer, Miss Josephine Lewis suffered an anaphylaxis reaction, rhinitis and urticaria. Miss Lewis had a known allergy to rice products. Miss Lewis is an asthmatic. The severe reaction resulted in hospitalisation. She remained an in-patient for five days and on High Dependency for 48 hours. Although she has not suffered lasting physical impairment, she has been diagnosed with Post-traumatic Stress Disorder. She receives medication to alleviate some symptoms. She is fearful of supermarkets and going out. Barbara Drapper was found guilty and given a suspended sentence of 2 years following mitigation, psychological reports, and as a

reflection of her previous exemplary character.

Further offences followed whilst Barbara Drapper was on probation, including a variation on the previous *modus operandi* which involved adding green and blue food dye to products procured in the manner stated above – to discolour and warn a consumer to avoid eating them. Barbara Drapper was not arrested until after the campaign had escalated significantly. She was found guilty of adding washing up liquid to the cocktail injected into pre-packaged convenience foods. She was caught after the 48 incidents and charged with actual bodily harm following a purchaser – Mr Edward Merton, 78, eating a *Worth It* extra value Cornish pasty in Tenby, Wales that had been tampered with, spent fourteen days in hospital with gastric disorder. Mr Merton has made a full recovery. A number of similar offences occurred across the UK during Barbara Drapper's probationary period and after she was arrested and placed on remand. Currently the total numbers 183 incidents. Barbara Drapper pleaded guilty to 48 of these and denies she has ever added iron filings, pins, glass or a laxative to foods and returning them to a supermarket shelf for sale. There is no evidence of her involvement in these very serious variations of the above offences.

Barbara Drapper presented with mental and physical ailments on remand at HMP Starling. She was transferred to the hospital wing and then on for tests. She was diagnosed with cancer of the colon. She has elected to refuse medical interventions for this condition. She transferred to Terrington House secure unit for further psychiatric testing before sentencing.

4. Barbara's computer hard drive was interrogated by the police. Initial reports indicate that Barbara accessed a variety of information pertinent to the planning and execution of her campaign. She was aware that evidence on the computer could be incriminating, but made no attempt to dispose of it.

5. Evidence from Barbara's computer, camper van and forensic results confirm that she was engaged in a campaign two years ago to encourage Worth It to improve their ecological stance by reducing the amount of packaging used on their products. This involved a letter writing campaign to her local store in the retail park at Brayston; to neighbouring Worth It stores; their Head Office and to the Prime Minister and Minister of the Environment.

6. It is believed that Barbara began, whilst writing the letters, to plan the much more complex campaign to change the buying habits of consumers.

7. She lost 26kg in weight, but concealed the fact from relatives and friends. She changed her hairstyle. She purchased a wig before radically restyling and changing hair colour. She bought a camper van, created a cover story for friends and family that she was taking a painting holiday in South Wales, and left to tour the country and action her campaign.

8. Barbara kept an extensive record on her computer and a hard copy of the responses to her actions. She kept files of press cuttings and added her own comments in margins to extended articles and analysis. She posted responses to certain blogs on the Internet and regularly contributed comments regarding *Worth It* to The Companions of Creation website.

9. In October of this year she was apprehended at her home in Brayston.

10. Since being sentenced to a custodial sentence, Barbara has refused to talk to the police, or her solicitor in any great detail. She has described herself as a political prisoner.

Education and Employment:

Barbara grew up in Ledding in Wellingbridgeshire. Her father was a railway worker and her mother was a housewife. She has one sister, three years her senior - Doreen. Barbara followed her older sister to Greta Courtney Girls School. She achieved seven 'O' Levels in English Language, English Literature, History, Biology, Chemistry, Physics and Art.

Barbara left school at 16 and attended Ledding Technical College, taking a secretarial course (September 1961). Barbara left the course just before Christmas because she did not wish to become a secretary. She worked temporarily in a shoe shop and a chemist before beginning her training as a State Registered Nurse in September 1962.

Barbara qualified at Ledding General in 1964. She continued to work at the hospital in General Medical for a further 6 years. After the birth of her daughter in 1971, Barbara took a break for four years, returning to part-time employment at the hospital and occasional agency work in 1975. She continued with this pattern of employment until 1986 when she became a Practice Nurse in a Brayston Medical Practice. Barbara retired in 2004.

Family Situation:

Barbara is a widow. She lives alone. Her sister, Doreen, lives fifteen miles away. Doreen is married to Robert (Rob). They have a small dog breeding and kennel business.

Psychiatric History:

Barbara has a history of mild depression. Following the birth of her daughter, Jennifer, in November 1971, Barbara was diagnosed with Post-natal depression by Dr Alan Bridger, Cromer Road Practice, Brayston in February 1971. In 1978 following a late miscarriage, Barbara was prescribed Valium. She remained on Valium at 20mg a day for twelve and a half months (Dr Michael Andrewson, Cromer Road Practice, Brayston, March 1979). In 2001 her father, Reginald Green, died of a heart attack. Barbara took a month off work and was diagnosed with stress (Dr Janet Sall, Cromer Road Medical Practice, Brayston June 2001). She had no formal medication but joined a group therapy session for six sessions run by Crying For Them Charity. In May 2002, her husband, Derek Drapper died in a road traffic accident; the accident was caused by his heart attack. Three months later, Barbara was diagnosed with mild depression (Dr Janet Sall, Cromer Road Medical Practice, Brayston, August 2002) and Sertraline was prescribed beginning at 20mg twice a day. She stayed on a maintenance dosage of 40mg a day for 7 months and then stopped taking the drug without further discussion with her GP. In December 2003, her only child, Jennifer, died from breast cancer, aged 34. Jennifer was married and had two young children. In November 2005, her former son-in-law Alan married again and moved to Longhellington with Barbara's two grandchildren, Natalie and Matthew.

Past Medical History:

Barbara had measles, mumps and chicken pox as a child. She had her tonsils removed when she was 9.

Barbara gave birth to a healthy baby girl in November 1971.

She had a miscarriage at approximately 24 weeks in December 1978.

Hypertension (June 2003).

Medication on Admission

25mg Asprin

2.5mg Bendroflumethiazide

Hamish MacAllister

Mental State on Admission:

Barbara was casually dressed and appeared clean and tidy. She was co-operative but made no eye contact. She created rapport through answering general questions and reminiscing about hospital life. Her manner was reserved and measured. She presented non-verbal signals of possible agitation: she repeatedly fiddled with her wedding ring. She sat for most of the time in a posture, sitting forward. Her speech was clear and articulate. She denied being in a low mood. She expressed concern for her grandchildren and her own future.

Hamish MacAllister

Physical Examination:

Cardiovascular, respiratory, gastrointestinal and neurological examinations proved unremarkable.

Hamish MacAllister

Nursing Report:

Height on admission: 1.65m

Weight on admission: 80.5kg

Height on discharge: 1.65m

Weight on discharge: 77kg

Goals on Admission:

1. Fitness to plead. Court Report.
2. Identify a diagnosis, if appropriate.
3. Carry out appropriate risk assessments.
4. Help Barbara assess her future needs.
5. Help Barbara to explore her motivation and past actions.

Incidents:

7th October	Refused to eat lunch. 'Not hungry'.
9th October	Request for organic diet on grounds of personal beliefs.
10th October	Refused to attend session with psychiatrist.

11th -14th Oct	Refused to speak for whole day.
14th October	Refused all food.
15th October	Refused all food.
16th October	Refused prescribed medication. Refused all food.
23rd October	Organic bread and soup eaten.
29th October	Refused to attend group therapy.
2nd November	Refused to talk to Detective Sergeant Talbot.
7th November	Refused to join in at occupational therapy.
10th November	Refused to speak to psychologist.
15th November	Uncooperative during significant parts of session with psychologist.
20th November	Threw plates of food at wall.
23rd November	Sit in began in room.
27th November	Sit in ended.

Patient Relationships:

Barbara has kept herself to herself for much of the time. She has not spent significant time with other patients. She was compliant, attending group sessions initially and then refused to continue to attend. Barbara refused to attend occupational therapy, but asked for an assessment to use the gym.

Recommendations:

Barbara presents as withdrawn into herself for significant periods of time. Conversation and social contact appear to exhaust her.

She will need to:

1. Explore issues of grief and anger.
2. Develop, with assistance, strategies to engage confidently and become more socially involved.
3. Explore therapeutically her avoidance and withdrawal.

Adrian Wallace

Psychiatric Nurse

Terrington House

Psychological Assessment Report

Ruth Gould

Psychologist in Clinical Training

Dates of Assessment:

30th August, 3rd September, 6th September, 20th September, 22nd September, 28th September.

Introduction:

At the time of this assessment Barbara is an in-patient at Terrington House, St. Margaret's Hospital, Wellingbridge.

Presentation during assessment:

Barbara was very willing to attend sessions to begin with when we were covering background information: setting the scene for the assessment. During the final two weeks of the assessment period, nursing staff reported and I witnessed Barbara highly agitated at the prospect of further sessions. She chose to shut herself away in her room.

Barbara was able to self-calm on these occasions. Although she did not attend one session until three quarters of an hour after the appointment; when she did attend she chose to stay for a few minutes only.

Barbara was a very willing conversationalist about her childhood and her professional life as a nurse. She was interested in how some tests worked and their purpose, diagnostically.

Psychometric Assessment:

The Hugenot-Cohen Executive Function Diagnostic System (HCEFDS) is a selection of tasks designed to assess executive functioning. This includes working memory, planning cognitive flexibility (the ability to shift between different paradigms or rules) and inhibitory control. The HCEFDS conclusions are assimilated under the following test headings:

Sequence Pattern Marking

This task assesses cognitive flexibility, working memory and sustained attention. It also includes a control test for motor speed.

Barbara was able to pick out numbers from groups; connect sequences; and process number and letter patterns. Barbara had no problems with motor speed.

Word Fluency

This test assesses generative ability and cognitive flexibility.

Barbara showed some difficulty in switching between categories at the highest functioning levels which indicates that she may have a lack of cognitive flexibility in her decision-making.

Design Awareness Fluency

This test assesses generativity in the non-verbal domain. It also assesses cognitive flexibility.

Barbara exhibited slightly below average ability to switch between filled and empty dots. This indicates that she may have a slight deficit in cognitive shifting. She had no problems in initiating designs. She made many attempts with some errors.

Word-Colour Interference

This is a test of inhibitory control (the inhibition condition) and cognitive flexibility (inhibition/switching condition). It also includes control tasks involving naming and reading.

Barbara performed excellently in the control tasks. She had slightly more difficulty in switching between conditions, indicating that cognitive flexibility might be slightly impaired. She had an elevated error rate in the inhibition task which indicates a degree of impulsivity.

Sorting

This task measures cognitive flexibility as well as conception formation skills.

Barbara showed an above average ability in these tasks. She had short completion times which may indicate some impulsivity.

Questions – Yes or No?

This test requires that the person holds in mind information whilst acquiring and integrating new knowledge.

Barbara remained well motivated throughout. She achieved a very high ratio of correct to incorrect answers.

Office Block

This task measures planning, working memory and inhibitory control.

Barbara exhibited average spatial planning skills. She started quickly but then gave time for consideration. This indicates impulsivity but may also indicate a difficulty with maintaining attention.

Intelligence Quotient

Barbara scored 112 and is of above average intelligence.

The Beck Depression Inventory (BDI-II)

The Beck Depression Inventory is one of the most commonly used outcome measures to demonstrate treatment efficacy and monitor treatment progress for depressed patients.

Agitation

Barbara exhibited a well above average level of agitation.

Worthlessness

Barbara scored averagely for worthlessness.

Concentration

Barbara repeatedly drew attention to her difficulties in concentrating and the fact that she had "lost the thread". This was borne out in slightly below average scoring.

Weight Loss

It has been noted that during her in-patient assessment, Barbara has lost significant weight.

Somatic Preoccupation

Negligible.

Appetite Loss

Barbara has refused to eat non-organic foods.

Sleep Loss

Barbara has noted poor sleep patterns.

The Bunnie PI-R

The Bunnie PI-R test is a 20-item symptom related rating scale designed to assess psychopathic (antisocial) personality disorders in forensic groups.

The outcomes are based on responses to the semi-structured interview and on a review of collateral information.

Evidenced Biased Assessment:

History:

Barbara's personal history prior to the offending behaviour does not indicate previous violence against other people or suicidal behaviour. Background checks reveal no convictions or relevant information. There is no evidence of a taxonomy of rootlessness in her lifestyle choices. She has resided at the same address since her marriage in 1966 and has worked consistently in medical care as a SRN and later as a Medical Practice Nurse. There is no evidence in her medical record of a poor compliance with treatment or avoidance of mental health aftercare. On the contrary, she sought advice appropriately from her General Practitioner when suffering from depression. She took the drugs and advice as prescribed.

There are no contributing factors in her social background which would be indicative of promoting violence nor is there recorded evidence of any substance abuse.

It is reasonable to suggest however, that in recent years Barbara has experienced acute stress as a result of the deaths of her father, husband and daughter. In addition, the recent remarriage of her former son-in-law has resulted in her grandchildren moving to a new area, some distance from Barbara's home. This too has represented a significant bereavement, as has retirement.

The impact of this grief on a person who values family relationships, routine and order cannot be underestimated.

Conclusions:

Barbara is of well above average intelligence. She is not cognitively flexible and has difficulty in changing conditions swiftly.

There are significant indicators that Barbara shows no psychopathic or socio-psychopathic tendencies. There is evidence that she has had in the past and is now suffering from severe depression.

Ruth Gould

Clinical Psychologist in Training

Violence Risk Assessment

Annie Bute

Psychiatric Social Worker

Jessica Arkwright

Psychotherapist

Sessions:

5th September, 10th September, 18th September

Using the World Health Organisation Guidelines we assessed the potential risk of violence.

(Andrews and Jenkins (2000) *Managing Mental Disorders*)

Anger at Other People:

Barbara was able to express her anger against the business consortium that own Worth It supermarket chain. Anger against 'people in general' because they 'are blind to the risk they run every time they eat this rubbish', but no anger directed against other individuals. Her anger is focused on what Barbara sees as unjust systems which give people little or no choice and 'force feed' them foods which are killing them, and the people they love, prematurely.

Are you thinking about hurting anyone?

Barbara said she couldn't 'hurt a fly' *intentionally*. She was curt and aggressive when we brought up the incident with Miss Lewis and the other 47 incidents which she pleaded guilty to.

Barbara was adamant that she had faced the fact that if she did undertake this 'work' there could be 'collateral damage', but 'the worst case scenario' she had imagined was a child choking for a second or two on the rice paper. She had been 'devastated' by what had happened particularly 'other people jumping on the band wagon', but at least 'everyone now knew about the poisons in food'. On this basis, Barbara felt her behaviour had been justifiable.

Barbara admitted during the final session that she had considered committing suicide when she first heard the news abut Miss Lewis on the radio. She had considered harming herself again when she was taken into custody but said she was 'too much of a coward'. She realised then she had to do so much more for the good of the planet and that if that meant hurting some to help many, then so be it.

<u>When do you think you might hurt yourself or others?</u>

Barbara was very distressed that we had not 'taken in' that she could not and would not hurt anyone intentionally and that these folk were just the casualties of the campaign, not intentional assaults. We reminded her of the possibility she might harm herself. Barbara would not talk further about her own thoughts of suicide in session.

<u>Are you able to control the thoughts of hurting yourself?</u>

Barbara said she was still alive so she must be able to.

<u>Do you think you will be able to stop yourself from hurting yourself if you wanted to?</u>

Barbara was sure that she could.

<u>How long do you think you can control your thoughts about hurting yourself?</u>

Barbara did not comment. We would be cautious in our assessment at this point and suggest that she may have little control when faced with highly intrusive thoughts with regards to self-harm.

<u>How close have you come to hurting yourself in the past?</u>

Again, Barbara would not communicate regarding this area of the assessment. Our sense is that she may not have allowed herself to fully face her darkest and most negative thoughts and had underplayed their significance to herself and others in the past.

<u>History:</u>

Given Barbara's non-violent history and past successful social integration, the indicators are that she may now be suffering from severe depression. There could be a case made that she meets some of the clinical criteria for a sociopath. Although there is evidence of impulsivity and significant anger in her recent offending behaviours, the level of intent has genuinely been to consciousness raise amongst the general public rather than to inflict lasting harm on individuals within society.

Her *active voice* is primarily concerned with the injustice of the hand life has dealt her; the impact she believes diet has on healthy living; the culpability of those who sell to consumers irresponsibly and the injustice of her 'imprisonment'.

Barbara does not have a highly developed inner emotional landscape. She is non-empathetic with regards to her behaviour. She prefers focusing on 'doing' rather than reflecting on the impact of what will be or has been done. In this sense it is her *passive* voice which speaks of 'collateral damage' but cannot relate that empathetically to the potential impact her actions may have on another.

Conclusion:

Barbara does not pose a risk to society as a violent person. She is however at potential risk of self-harming.

Jessica Arkwright

Psychotherapist

Sessions: weekly and continuing as an out-patient.

I have attached various extract transcriptions from sessions as these are extremely helpful in evaluating the mental state of Barbara.

Barbara presented as an affable and chatty person with a clear value system, and good recall of past events.

Barbara has a strong dislike of being laughed at or humiliated.

Although she has remained silent regarding her deepest feelings about the many deaths in her family, she is well able to relate key events and has a gift for telling her own story in a compelling and engaging manner. She often uses her skill at drawing the listener into her world as a way of deflecting questions and comments. She finds maintaining such a high degree of control costly. Staff on the ward have noted that she often sleeps a great deal and complains of exhaustion. When alert she is watchful. She rarely shows concern for others. She is highly vigilant.

There is a sense in which following the significant emotional trauma of recent years, Barbara has attempted to channel feelings that she may find difficult to name and quantify into tangible activities. This has had the effect of making her feel safer and rather more in control of challenging events.

Barbara's inner emotional life is stark and this may well be as a result of compounded grief or it may point to a systemic dysfunction; at this stage, it would be purely speculative to comment.

Barbara is currently unable to take full responsibility for her actions or acknowledge empathetically the cost her actions may have caused another. She will need significant therapeutic assistance to slowly rebuild her emotional confidence and assertiveness in constructive and personally fulfilling ways.

Medication

Hamish MacAllister

Registrar

On admission, Barbara was on 75mg Aspirin and 2.5mg Bendroflumethiazide. During her in-patient assessment she has begun Citalopram at 20mg a day increasing to 40mg and at discharge will be increasing again to 60mg.

Barbara has presented as significantly anxious and attempts to mask much of her anxiety with activity, particularly talking. She will suddenly feel exhausted and sleep for long periods.

In addition we recommend continued intensive psychotherapy to explore her grief.

Clinical Diagnosis

Ishmael Maharinjiti

Consultant

AXIS I	Severe situationally induced depression
AXIS II	Reactive attachment disorder
AXIS III	Hypertension
AXIS IV	IQ in above average range

Treatment Plan

The Multidisciplinary Team recommends:

1. Barbara will continue to be seen by Dr Arkwright.
2. Barbara poses no risk to wider society but will need on-going psychiatric support and supervision with a Community Psychiatric Nurse/HMP Psychiatric Services.
3. Barbara challenges society's assumptions about itself and what is important; this makes her uncomfortable to listen to. Her behaviour can be challenging. There is no evidence of an underlying psychosis or pathology.

Ishmael Maharinjiti

Consultant, Adult Psychiatric Services

Canalside Cottage,
Chandler's Lane,
Wynleigh,
Brayston BY3 2PG

My Dear Babs,

Thank you for your long and encouraging letter. I hope you won't take this the wrong way but you do sound as though you have turned a corner. Your therapist – Jessica – sounds a good sort – and full of commonsense. I was particularly pleased to hear that the antidepressants and the antipsychotics had "Kicked in". They sound as though they have made a huge difference and are just the ticket. I know you are the last person to be a fan of drug interventions but you know, sometimes our bodies do need a hand to work at their optimum level.

Yes, I am sorry that I did "go on a bit" in my last letter. Writing is such an inadequate way to communicate, but I do understand you not wanting me to visit even at the open prison because you still don't feel up to it. I know I would find it hard to see you in that context – so I thank you for what I am sure is your sensitivity.

Bella had a short trip to the vet at the end of last week. She has the beginnings of arthritis. Nothing serious – and it is really only noticeable when we have been on a long-ish hike and she starts to stiffen up in the hours that follow. The vet, a new young woman from Hungary, has prescribed anti-inflammatories – and I'm to take her back for a check-up in a month. She seems fine on them and eats them like a treat at the end of her walk with a handful of food. She does love going into the forest for her free run. I'm finding as we both get a little older that we seem to match each other's pace well. She's never far from me when she's off chasing the odd rabbit or snuffling for smells. She's looking as good as new really apart from a few grey hairs on her muzzle which look awfully distinguished.

Bella was a huge hit last month at the church's pet service. She was one of five golden retrievers and Grace (Rector) asked if they could all come up together for a blessing! It caused a smile around the congregation – they all looked like the entries in a dog show! As far as I'm concerned, and I am sure you will agree, she was by far the most attractive golden retriever there!

I am off to Crete next week with Fiona and Ruth for a fortnight's holiday – so try not to worry too much if there is a delay before my next letter – or three! I will send you a card though.

I have spoken to a very nice woman at the Alternative Healing Centre in Brayston, and as requested, she has given me two names of holistic healers. When I talked to her a little about you, she did say that she hoped you realised that having chemotherapy and radiotherapy could really do no harm given the fact that the cancer is 'live' in your system – and might even do a great deal of good alongside more holistic therapies. I pass this on to you as she asked. I am not nagging again – honest!

Her name is Annie Whittaker and she has identified:

John Brown, 12 During Avenue, Brayston

Anna-Louise Fenwick, The Glass House, Sturgeon's Lane, Brayston as two local holistic healers. Anna-Louise is also a trained psychotherapist.

John Brown is a retired librarian and has been a healer for thirty odd years. He retired to Brayston four years ago.

Anna-Louise works part-time for Lucy's, the cancer help centre attached to hospital. She's also happy to do visualisation and mindfulness – if that helps. I didn't ask what they were, I guessed you would be more than up to speed.

I can make an appointment when you decide which you want to go for – and we have a release date.

With love,

Geraldine   x

BASTARDS
PISS OFF
OUT OF MY
LIFE

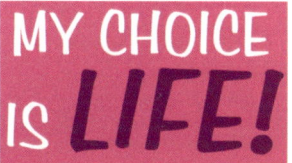

My Personal Journal

1st January

I've got to pull myself together.

<u>I WILL NOT GO ON LIKE THIS.</u>

New Year.

New start.

1. Lose weight.
2. I am not a victim.
3. I can take control.
4. I want to make a difference.

Weight:

110kg

Obese.

Bmi: 39.92 - almost clinically obese.

Hummmph.

Food Journal starts with what I am eating as I write:

1 cup of tea - skimmed milk.

3 Digestives now 5.

7pm Supper

2 lamb chops - have eaten these as I had them in the fridge. I will not waste food when millions are starving.

Peas, beans and boiled pots.

Resisted butter.

Apple.

8pm

Yoghurt - finishing up.

10pm Hot Choc - finishing up. But had to open the fresh jar to start finishing up. Stupid, I could have given this to Natalie. Will do this when I see her.

2nd January

Woke up at 2.30am. v. awake. Starving.

Had a banana.

Breakfast - 7am

Indigestion.

2 slices Toast with butter and honey.

Soothing.

Made list:

Need low fats prods.

Need to go to Worth It. Can't get this stuff at the Farmer's Market. More's the pity.

10am

Starving.

Grapes, apple, sultanas and a digestive (finishing up).

Not bought any more.

Managed a light and sensible lunch of salad and chicken.

Wanting to chew a pillow by 3pm. I have spent the day on the loo as I keep drinking to try and stave off the hunger. Need to find some other things to take my mind off eating.

Natalie wants a lift to the shops to meet her friends.

Hot choc in car and a bag of unsuitable food from the freezer.

Feel virtuous.

I will have to just drop her and leave the bag of goodies at theirs.

Not ready to walk past the wholefood Nuts place and Luke and Tracey's Food Hall just yet.

Still in cold turkey.

Can't paint - too hungry.

Can't clean - ditto.

No energy.

Sorry for myself.

Slept all afternoon.

4th January

Natalie and Matthew are getting ready for the return to school. So hard to see them doing this without their mum. They are very good. I forget that they had all those months when Jen was poorly. Alan is being a brick and is taking Natalie to get new shoes tomorrow.

I have found just doing a food diary is making me think before I eat.

Too much fruit gives me the runs.

7th January

Weight: 109.5 kg 109 if I lean back on the scales.

I will count this as 109kg. I need to believe in this.

Trying to get my head round my New Year resolutions.

Sat down to think. Afternoon seemed to disappear - nodded off no doubt - and no cup of tea waiting for me when I came to. How I miss Derek. None the wiser really following my efforts to GET MYSELF SORTED OUT. I have time on my hands but I don't seem to have the energy to do much with it.

Bungalow needs a blitz.

The loo is a disgrace and I can't see one half of the spare room under ironing.

I will try and do some SOON. Gentle exercise that counts and gets something done.

9pm. Coped with the ironing until I found a couple of T-shirts of Jen's. I must have brought them home to wash. God knows why.

I've not ironed them - put them in the bottom drawer in Jen's room. I know I should return them to Alan. I know I should. It's so silly but I just don't want to part with them just yet. I don't suppose he will miss them.

10th January

Coping better with feeling hungry. Find grazing healthy bits and bobs all through the day helps.

Jamie, Jen's Macmillan nurse, popped in to see Alan and the kids the other day.

I am pleased. Alan said he thought Jamie had helped the kids.

I HAVE FINISHED THE IRONING.

But now have washing hanging out.

What used to take a couple of hours seems to take days. I can't concentrate. I feel like I am wading through a minefield. Everything is tender. I don't want to do some things because of the memories. Funny, unexpected things seem to set me off and that's it, I can't do any more. Exhausted. Have decided to throw out an old tea towel - we bought it on holiday in Guernsey years back - but it is more holes than cotton these days. Sad. End of an era in a way. I can remember the holiday like it was yesterday, Jen would have only been about 6. We were on the beach a lot and Derek was busy making sand castles. We all played French cricket and one day, when we found we had real sand sandwiches because the dog had got to them - we each had two 99 ice cream cones to make up for it. I can still see Jen in her little red and white costume and Derek swinging her round and dipping her in the sea. You never think all that's important when you're in the middle of it - but it is.

I was thinking of Jen when she married. How determined she'd been to do things her way - and how miffed I was. Can't have been the first mum who thought her daughter could have done better for herself.

She was stubborn, not just the when and where - which was difficult enough because we weren't made of money and she wanted the full traditional spread - but the details - it was straight out of one of these Brides magazines and it had to be perfect or it wasn't worth doing at all.

To Jen
Without you
I am always looking
To see if you are coming

And as I'm going
I search the rear view mirror
On the off chance
That you aren't gone forever
But are waiting for my glance.

14th January

A **definite** 109kg. Maybe more lost. I am going to treat myself to a new set of scales.

15th January

108kg on new scales. <u>A good investment.</u>

Met my neighbour and she is going to a weight loss club in town.

No.

I think I would feel ridiculed having my weight shouted out and everyone clapping or sympathising. I bet I'd stop going the second I thought I wasn't actually losing weight - so what's the point in starting?

16th January

Couldn't sleep.

Natalie brought her friend Emily round for an old-fashioned tea. I'd made scones and a proper cake. Ate it too - and there's stuff left. I feel really fed up today. I think it was once the girls had gone. I don't suppose a couple of slices will do that much harm. <u>All homebaked.</u>

What has got into me? I am SO ANGRY. Why? What's anyone done to me? I read in a women's magazine the other day at the hairdresser's that "Life is what you make it". I smiled. Maybe that's it. My life is what other people have made it. I've never been in the driving seat - half the time I've not even been on board for the ride. Something has passed me by - I can't put my finger on it. Yes, people I love have gone. I ache not seeing them but the emptiness is so big; so much bigger than the ache; so much bigger than losing them - it's like I've lost out on life. It's like the ache is just the symptom and the emptiness is the illness. Nothing there - not just nothing left.

<u>What makes me angry</u>

1. Food that is processed and has additives and preservatives AND KILLS PEOPLE I LOVE AND LOADS OF OTHERS.
2. WHY ME?????
3. WHY CAN'T I JUST WALK AWAY and get over it????
4. Hoodies
5. People who do not say please.
6. FEELING EMPTY WHEN I USED TO FEEL FAR TOO FULL.

<u>21st January</u>

108kg. Weight - plateau - which is RIDICULOUS this early in my diet.

I could always tell at the surgery if the ladies were cheating!!!

I made too many scones and too big a cake because I WANTED to eat the leftovers. I need to get my head round this. Am I serious about losing weight? The problem is I don't seem to have the motivation these days. I could always shed a few pounds for a holiday or a big family do - but now there doesn't seem much point. I need to find the motivation from somewhere but feel so tired. I suppose it should be expected, she's not been gone a month.

I NEED TO DO SOMETHING WITH MY LIFE.

<u>22nd January</u>

Didn't sleep at all well last night so got up at 3.30am and sorted out the drawers where I keep all my old health leaflets, useful information from the paper and recipes. I filled a large sack with paper recycling and made a pile of recipes I can allow myself to use. When I go shopping I will get rid of the stuff and buy a large file to sort the recipes into. I saw one that is especially designed for recipes in the supermarket just the other day, it has wallets and is wipe clean.

I also made a list of what I am eating and when, this coming week.

Bonus: I will save money and throw less away too.

Found my teenage diary from when I was 15 - talk about laugh. I made a cuppa and settled in the armchair by the fire with my duvet for company and read it all the way through in one sitting - what a daft kid I was - all het up over nothing - with a complete sense of humour deficit. She made me really chuckle, my young self. I can't understand these people who say if they had half a chance they would go back to being a teenager again. Too much like hard work from what I can recall.

No meat,

Pulses,

Eggs,

Cheese - but low fat,

Brown rice,

Wholemeal pasta,

Fruit,

Salad,

Fish.

NO SWEET THINGS.

I CAN CHOOSE TO BE IN CONTROL.

23rd January

Trying not to make a thing out of the sleeping but it is starting to get to me. 2.30am. No sleep after that. Got up at 5.30am.

Sometimes I just run out of steam in the afternoon and then, of course, I nap. Come the night-time I am as wide awake as you like.

Ran into Janet Sall in the butcher's in town. She asked how I was. I said I was fine and heard that her eldest has just got his Duke of Edinburgh's.

She has asked me to pop in at the Medical Practice and make an appointment to see her.

I have decided the time has come to get rid of Derek's things. The "I am not a victim" thing. Well, I'm not. Keeping possessions doesn't replace my Derek. I feel rather ashamed of myself for holding on to so much for so long - others should have the benefit. I have looked at what needs to be done and made the beginnings of a list. I am disappointed in myself, but what's the point? I haven't *done any more despite giving my head a real ear-bashing.*

Alan has been an example. He, and a couple of Jen's friends - Alison and Steph have been through her clothes and sorted out what Natalie and Matthew would like to keep and bagged the rest for charity.

I think Steph has taken a couple of things as keepsakes.

No one asked if I wanted anything. No one. Why should I be surprised? Why should they? BECAUSE THEY DAMN WELL SHOULD. SHE WAS MY DAUGHTER BEFORE SHE WAS THEIR FRIEND OR LOVER.

Still I have the T-shirts and some lovely things from when Jen was just a girl.

What does it matter? It won't bring her back.

I can't think Natalie and Matthew will want anything of Derek's. It feels the wrong time to ask really. I'm sure Alan will think it is. I will box up some stuff for them, maybe some photos and letters and so on and leave it in the garage until the moment's right. I should think Matthew might like one of his grandpa's old flat caps - maybe Natalie too - you see girls wearing them too these days. Maybe a tie - something from his dressing table. I don't know. Maybe I should leave it. I don't want to upset anyone. Two wrongs and all that.

One bag of underpants to recycling. Maybe it should have been landfill.

24th January

ANOTHER BAD NIGHT.

Tetchy and fed up.

Bought a large packet of crisps when I went to get a paper. Managed half. Dying of thirst afterwards.

Don't like crisps as much as I once did.

Nothing seems in place somehow.

I've boxes all over the bedroom. My own fault. Sorting out. Recycling. Charity. Memory Boxes. Save. <u>All a bit much</u>. But the urge to sort is strong. I want some control, but feel helpless and like a lead lump most of the time.

I am going to just put everything in the spare room and shut the door.

I AM FED UP WITH THE LOT OF IT.

Am tempted to phone one of these house clearing firms and ask them to do the room. Felt I was being disloyal.

Have left it all. But I did rip up a load of old gardening plans and papers of Derek's. A rough sort of justice. That will teach him for not spending more time with me.

Saved some seeds, I expect they are well past being able to plant them, I know how they feel.

28th January

107 kg.

Rainbow trout and lots of watercress.

The carton of ice cream at the back of the freezer was the mistake. I have known it was there all along. But I couldn't go on turning a blind eye.

Bugger shoes. How can a man have so many shoes - some of them he must have had for years? How am I supposed to recycle old shoes for crying out loud?!

<u>What I should have told Derek</u>

1. You were mad to love me.
2. I missed you when you were out so much.
3. I didn't tell you I loved you often enough.
4. I should have told you not having another child didn't matter that much to me in the end.
5. I should have asked you how much it mattered to you.
6. I should have taken more of an interest in the things that mattered to you.
7. I should have told you that I'm sorry I couldn't be all you needed me to be.

<u>29th January</u>

Doreen and Rob came round this evening. I looked at the snaps of their holiday in Cyprus on Doreen's new laptop. Very posh it was too - the holiday and the computer. The live-in kennel hand (she can't be called a maid) Lila, is working out well apparently. She doesn't sound as though she does any more than our Derek used to do of an evening and at the weekend, but this young lass has a wage, room and paid holidays! Derek was always a bit soft when it came to dogs. Sometimes I think he preferred dogs and plants to people - even his own family! Lila has taught the dogs Polish apparently - but not Rob and Dor!

Doreen just hopes she stays. Apparently she's doing qualifications at the college one day a week and they are hoping to expand to include a grooming service on the back of some certificate she'll get in the summer.

Mind boggles.

They breed over-fed, indulged puppies and charge the earth for them. Why not save a stray and keep the money in the bank?!

Doreen looks a bit plump - and Rob. Brown but not raw. Have they any idea about melanoma?? They said they spent most of the time on trips and in quiet restaurants. No sun worshipping. Funny colour for staying in the shade??? Sprayed on? No sign on collar - must be a good preparation if it is.

They say they are popping in next week.

Apparently Dor's worried about me.

I AM NOT.

Nothing a good night's sleep won't cure.

I don't look pasty.

4th February

105kg.

No special food treats to celebrate. Bought a book instead. "Loving Yourself: Loving the Earth" by Wendy Kirkwood. Not a crystal in sight. All very practical and sensible. Up to page 20. Must also buy "Additive Attack" and "Destroying the Planet: the Outcome of Capitalism". Should help me sleep.

6th February

I am turning into a night owl. I actually went shopping in the MIDDLE OF THE NIGHT!

I met Geraldine there too! She is like a good angel that woman. I do like her. We are having coffee at Luigi's next week. I am treating myself to a new top to celebrate. I reckon I could squeeze into another size smaller.

I am now the proud owner of a laptop, scanner and printer - courtesy of Worth It. I resent them getting the money - really I do - but it was a planned impulse buy. Well, it was an impulse buy after two seconds planning. Even I could see their pricing was incredibly competitive after what Doreen said she'd paid for hers. It was a lot to find, and I don't suppose I will use it _that_ much - but I was very impressed with what Rob was doing on theirs.

Alan doesn't like me spoiling the kids - so I might as well spend it on something I can use. They'll use it when they visit. Doreen thinks I should take an Older holiday - they swear by them. To be honest, I think I'd just swear.

Not my cup of tea at all. I resent the money as much as anything. Having to be nice to strangers - ugh! Everyone wanting to know your business! If I had to go I would pretend to be someone else, just to get a bit of privacy. I NEED MY OWN SPACE.

Rob is coming over tomorrow night to set up and check I am safe in charge of a laptop and won't blow it up.

I have put the boxes containing all the equipment just inside the spare room. I shudder at all the packaging.

It's no good, I will have to do something about the spare room before Rob and Dor go in there. Dor will throw a pink fit. She will use it as evidence against me.

I am using it as evidence against me too.

I can get on with it when I can't sleep tonight.

Except - for some reason - I never do.

7th February

I now know how to switch on this computer and the printer and get into the word processing bit and also on line. I now have an e-mail address. It is barbaradrapper@earth.co.uk. Earthlove is a charity I have read about recently. They do e-mail addresses and have a great on-line shop.

I can surf.

I have shopped for earth mugs which say "save our planet not yourself".

I did some of all of this computer stuff at work, but I am out of practice. Badly. I found NHS Direct though so I was quite pleased.

Just like old times.

Dor says she is worried about me because of how I am keeping the house. She says it is a window into my emotional state. I told her that was a lot of tosh. She says I am not looking after myself. I thanked her for her concern. She may be my sister but she can be a silly bitch sometimes. She wants to take a look at her own place before she takes a shot at *mine. I have never seen so much mud outside of the garden.*

Bessie, their youngest retriever has had a litter. Dor wants to give me one of the pups for my birthday. She tells me I need someone to look after.

I could murder a digestive or sixteen! The last thing I need is another bitch to look after.

<u>*11th February*</u>

First entry on the computer.

Big moment.

104kg

Now I don't know what to say.

The computer feels a bit intimidating.

I am going to call it Freddie – less scary with a name.

Went to the library this morning and got a book out on how to understand computers if you are stupid. It's good. I am stupid.

I could really get into this surfing business.

I have had e-mails from Rob, Alan (at work), Natalie (at school and at home) Matthew (at home) and Marian at the surgery – I couldn't resist telling them I was now on line.

I have found Jen's Woodland Burial Site website and have marked it in favourites. I like being able to put a picture up of the woodland and gardens in the evening. The Cemetery in Brayston just has a site address so I can't put

Derek's resting place up on the screen as well. What exactly is Broadband? Is it safe to use?

12th February

Met Geraldine for a coffee. It was lovely to see her again. It felt odd meeting and it not being at Worth It. We seemed, I don't know, companionable. I can't say what we talked about. Nothing very heavy. The weather – grey and wet today – but not cold. The packaging campaign. G. said that quite a few people in The Mothers' Union at Brayston Church were joining in too. She said even her Rector was!

She told me a bit about her life. She's a retired Headmistress from a girl's independent school. You'd never know it just talking to her. She's very approachable and not at all stuck up. She didn't ask why I had been crying when we last met. I was pleased about that. We will meet at Luigi's next week. I wonder if G. is lonely?

Meeting her makes me realise I probably am. It was lovely to have something to look forward to and get dressed up for.

I am now on PhizogMag and PeopleDirect – social networking sites. Phizog is especially for ecological stuff.

13th February

Geraldine mentioned something about the packaging campaign having a website.

I don't seem to have been to sleep for <u>three</u> days.

A WHOLE NEW WORLD has opened up before me. I have not only found the packaging website G. mentioned – but so many other things – you just would not believe.

In the last 22 hours – and <u>37 mins</u> I have:

1. *joined Companions of Creation and bought a book about recycling and a badge and a car sticker from them. I have read loads of articles about recycling and land fill. Shocking.*

2. *found a healthy eating chat room and I am signed in as Bulgebattler. I was pleased with that. I thought of the names Matthew gives his characters when he is playing games and made one up based on them. I chatted to 'Fluffypinkgirliegirl' who turned out to be a transsexual awaiting the op' and 'Fightfatforgood' who has had three babies in five years and is struggling to get her weight down. It was just like being back at the surgery. Fightfatforgood really just needed a bit of hand holding, let's face it, who wouldn't with lots of little ones under your feet all day.*

3. *found a diet site with stuff to buy to help slim. Not happy to try chemicals – but I liked the idea of the plate to limit the size of your portions. I have ordered this and a pack of seaweed patches. I have printed out loads about Hoodia too. Also colonic irrigation and fitness. Just because I know what you should do doesn't mean I do it.*

4. *found a site about caring for a puppy. Do I want a dog? I haven't had one since I was a child – Rufus. Don't think I do – but I have printed out some sheets to show Doreen and Rob that I have given some thought to their suggestion and not just dismissed it out of hand.* **_I do not want the added responsibility._** *It's exhausting enough looking after me. At least if they see I have done some research they will know that I am absolutely clear why this is not a runner – and I am. I need a dog like a hole in the head.*

5. *looked at what the bungalow is worth. Not sure why. Just found myself in a property search and decided to look. I think I accidentally signed up for some sort of*

valuation – but I will bar the front door if anyone actually comes knocking.

6. *found a local-ish place that might be up to recycling some of Derek's tools. I haven't even started on the garage, but there's a lot that could be of use to someone and this charity sends stuff to developing countries.*

7. *sent e-mails to the grandkids and Alan.*

8. *found Geraldine's church website. A bit go ahead for me. What is feminist theology when it's at home? Something to do with Germaine Greer? Note to ask Geraldine. Seems to me they are very into sustainability. Not sure why that surprises me. I guess I've always thought Christians were all a bit like our Doreen – out of touch with reality.*

9. *joined www.findyouroldbuddy.com. Found my old school and have sent e-mails to 3 old girl friends. I counted up the number of years since I saw them and it's unbelievable. It may not be such a good idea to be in touch – but there's no harm in trying. A lot of water under the bridge and all that.*

10. *Tired but can't think of sleeping. Settle down and within half an hour I can feel myself grinding my teeth and wide awake – almost defying my brain to switch off.*

Need to go shopping and then I will start on getting the boxes from the spare room into the car. Time to let things go and truly become the Queen of Recycling!

17th February

I have had hardly a minute to get on. There is so much to learn. I have been looking at some studies for weight reducing drugs and also studies on the negative impact of dieting. I am now getting alerts in my inbox from Companions of Creation and have joined three other ecological campaigns. I have spent this afternoon writing letters. It's all very easy – they provide the pro forma.

I can't believe that all these reports are out there about pollution and sustainability and people are not doing anything about it. Am I the only person in the world with a computer? Am I the only person who takes the time to read? Kill ourselves with additives and suffocate the planet with pollution! There has to be another way. I have posted a reply on Green Dream about supermarkets exploiting consumers and having a responsibility to us to keep us informed about food that is unhealthy and a person called Jez and another called Jelliebean have written in after me to say they agree. Jez encourages civil disobedience. I can't quite see what that has to do with anything. People have got to eat.

One e-mail from old school friend. Beverley is also a widow! She lives near Cardiff now. I have chatted a bit – but lost heart. Couldn't be doing for some reason. Everything I wanted to say was all doom and gloom.

Natalie came over after school today with Matthew as Alan has to go to some works dinner tonight. He is picking them up on his way home. I said they were more than welcome to stay over – but he insisted. Natalie asked if she could spend time looking at Jen's things in her old bedroom. They are very alike. Matt wants me to buy "Star Raider Explodes III" so he can play it at mine. I will have to ask Alan if this all right with him.

18th February

*Alan arrived to pick the children up at **2am**! I was sure he'd had a serious accident. The children were wilting by 10 – and so I tucked them up on the settee and armchair with the footstool with a drink of milk. I put old 78s on the player and* *they dozed while I went on-line. Alan is normally quite responsible – sometimes a bit over protective as far as the kids are concerned. I eventually plucked up the courage to try his mobile but it was switched off. At midnight I tried the mobile again. Still no reply, but I left a message. I even tried ringing him at home. I was so sure something had happened to him.*

12.30pm Took my mobile into the kitchen and with my heart in my mouth phoned the local A & E. No reported RTAs near here. They told me to calm down and not to worry. Police said he was probably enjoying himself and had lost track of time. Usually Alan is so particular – he gives me all the details of where he is and how to contact him if there's an emergency. He <u>always</u> leaves his mobile on. Terribly worried.

2am I could have thrown my arms round his neck and kissed him, I was that relieved. Played it down. Asked if he had had a nice time. He apologised for being so late – he hadn't realised the time. The children were out for the count – so we decided to leave them where they were – seemed for the best. Alan decided he'd rather sleep in his own bed at home so set off – but showed me his mobile was on before he left.

8.30am I am sure I would have been as grumpy as hell after a night on the settee – but they thought it was a sleepover! Pancakes for breakfast and we watched cartoons for a bit until their Dad came to pick them up – looking a bit sheepish I have to say. I think it is lovely that he could go out and enjoy himself and lose track of time for once.

I ate 2 pancakes and felt quite ill.

I am too tired today to do much.

104kg.

I need to exercise more – but too tired to face it.

Frightened myself last night.

20*th* February

Alan has asked if it would be possible for Natalie and Matthew to come for a sleepover at the weekend. Apparently there's a good chance of some promotion if he can attend some conference. When Jen was well he was always off here, there and everywhere – trade fairs, promotions or motivational weekends. I thought they sounded like he had joined some sort of cult!

Makes no odds to me as long as I know how to get hold of him and WHERE he is. I would enjoy the company.

The Landings Country House Hotel,

Bellton on the Water.

V, smart.

Looked at their website. V. expensive. Alan must be on the up.

Had the courage of my convictions last night and decided to follow some leads I had found a while back linking cancer and cardiovascular stuff to additives and chemicals used in food manufacture and preservation. V. upsetting.

How come we don't get told ALL THIS???? We are slowly being poisoned by food companies and pesticide companies. Don't get me started on GM.

Is it possible there is such a thing as organic anymore?

21*st* February

Met Geraldine for lunch a Luigi's. G. is planning a holiday. She is going to see some Shakespeare at Stratford with some other ex-teachers. She says she loves it but is always glad to get home. They are going after Easter. I have no Easter plans. She nudged me to think about something I would really like to do. I am sorry to say my mind went a complete blank. I wanted to do what G. expects of me. She seems so positive about my future.

G. has suggested lunch at her house next week. She is a member of Companions of Creation too. Apparently it will be Lent so no pudding just fruit! Shame. I don't think it should count if someone else gives it to you to eat. Still if it's Lent. It's Lent.

25th February

102 kg.

I think this weight loss is because my feet haven't touched the ground. I had forgotten what hard work it is to have the grandchildren around for an extended stay. It seemed much easier when I was over at theirs – they have all their familiar things to hand and they know the house rules. Natalie and I had a little disagreement about using the phone without asking – and then I was very taken aback because she had put on one of her mother's T-shirts she'd found in Jen's old room. For a split second it could have been Jen standing there. I shouted at her to take it off. She was confused and hurt and upset. She had put it in on to please me and show off a bit I think. I couldn't find the words to tell her that I am missing Jen too. I did my best to patch things up, but we skirted round each other a bit after that. Matt just kept his head down.

Alan arrived. We had just finished playing "Blink and You'll Miss It" and the children had eaten a whole large packet of popcorn. I was bushed. Alan looked quite chipper and wasn't full of his usual grumbles about the conference being a waste of time. He bought me some chrysanthemums to say thank you for having the children and a box of Belgian

Truffles. He hadn't remembered about the diet or that I hate chrysanthemums just like Jen. Thought that counts.

Early night.

3am. I am worried about Alan, Natalie and Matthew's health. It may be too late for me. But they have to stop poisoning their bodies.

NOW. I have to stop encouraging them to.

27th February

Natalie arrived in a bad state. She had had a weird text from Dad. It just said something about missing her and not being able to wait to see her. I said I thought it was OK for Dad to feel sad when she was at school. Maybe he was having a really tough day at work and wished he was at home with her and Matthew. She looked at me a bit old fashioned – like I am slow. I think she is now officially ADOLESCENT.

28th February

Matthew has decided he wishes to be known from now on as Matt. I have always preferred it!!!!!! ☺

1st March

Matt's birthday and party. He had a large number of children from school attending. I tried to count them – but became confused as many of them were dressed as Time Lords, aliens and Superheros. There was an awful lot of running around and charging up and down stairs and round and round the garden. So many piles of smallish boys fighting each other and squirming on the ground. I was quite glad, retrospectively, that I had a daughter.

Alan had booked a chap from work to entertain them. He played old-fashioned parlour games. I would have thought these modern young would be far too sophisticated for all that nonsense, but they lapped it up. Then he did a bit of magic with Matt as his helper and produced the cake for tea. It wasn't quite wizards and witches though, I think Matt was fairly unimpressed. Several of the parents stayed around and I noticed Alan had organised wine and nibbles for all the grown-ups in the conservatory. It smelt like a pub in there. I couldn't imagine Jen agreeing to this. I managed to open the windows and just hoped most of them weren't driving home. Jen was very particular about adults not drinking significantly in front of children.

It was nice to see Steph and Alison. Also Sue and Debbie from Jen's work. Sue's son is the same age as Matt – so he came for the party anyway. Steph bought Matt a DVD. Alison had splashed out on what looked like a very expensive MP3 player. I know a lot of them are more glamorous than good quality these days and they're probably all made in China, but even so. This was a name brand. I couldn't help but notice that Alan looked really chuffed with the gift. I have always been severely reprimanded for buying expensive gifts. My computer game looked rather paltry by comparison. I suppose Alison does earn fairly good money these days – so why not? She and Dave haven't been blessed with children as yet.

Matt was in floods of tears by 9.30pm and sick by 10.15pm. Cleared up and tucked up – he was fine. He suddenly looked 5 again. I am exhausted. Maybe I will sleep better tonight.

4th March

I have been exercising each day – just walking faster and further.

RESULT.

100kg

But not much sleep.

5th March

I am getting more and more concerned about the things I am reading on the net.

Apparently there are over 14,000 different chemical compounds that have been developed as additives to improve the colour or preserve our food longer. We are exposed to these additives from conception, but human bodies are not meant to be exposed in this way. They cause our bodies to malfunction.

Not all additives are bad.

Some additives are cancerous.

Foods that have been pickled increase the risk of cancer of the stomach and oesophagus. Problems to investigate further:

Nitrosamines.

Smoking and barbecuing foods.

Heterocyclic amines.

Acrylamide

Aromatase.

*I do wonder about Jen. Even Derek. Could what they ate have affected their life chances significantly? I think the answer is a definite **YES**.*

6th March

Went to Geraldine's for lunch. Talked to her about my research. She is a knowledgeable person and I didn't want to appear stupid. We sort of stopped eating part way through the quiche. She had questions and got up at one point and started rummaging through the cardboard packaging for various foods she had eaten and we quickly saw just how many contained additives which are dangerous.

G told me that she tries to eat a lot of organic food but she still has concerns about what the Soil Consortium are now saying they think is acceptable in terms of insecticide and other chemical use on organic soil. She thinks the only answer is to grow our own. I said that Derek had wanted to do that – but somehow his heart was more in flowers.

G gave me the name of Green Man Organic Boxes at Upper Treland. They don't have a website – but I got a girl on the phone and have ordered a weekly box. The smallest. I hope you can stop the boxes coming if you need to.

G and I are going to meet at the Farmer's Market in Brayston at 8.30am on Saturday morning. She is e-mailing me a draft letter which we are going to deliver to all the dairy and meat stallholders asking them to think about low fat produce. She's determined is Geraldine!

7th March

Dropped in on Dor and Ron. Dutifully admired six puppies that all looked pudgy and sleepy to me apart from one who simply screamed the place down. Never heard such a racket.

8th March

On the internet last night. I will catch up with sleep later. Shocking research on the links between additives and stomach and bowel cancer/other diseases. It's a big, dark secret and the supermarkets are colluding – so are the fast food outlets. Pages and pages on hydrogenated fats which have left me speechless and feeling sick. Humans can't digest these – but most fast food is cooked using them. It's cheap. It keeps the population down. Probably more effective than a major war.

I keep posting stuff on internet sites but the received wisdom is that it's a waste of time trying a paper campaign (not ecologically sound either says Jelliebean). The big supermarkets and food outlets have got the market stitched up. People would rather have convenience and cheap food – than quality food which hasn't been processed and which is safer to eat.

The producers grow it and process it cheaply and forget to tell us what they have added. Read this thing about how much water is pumped into chicken and also how many antibiotics – no wonder antibiotics don't work when prescribed.

I've read three library books on food and farming methods. Also a long article in the Sunday paper criticising food monopolies. In some parts of the country 60% of the people shop at Worth It at least once a week.

Natalie has a boyfriend. His name is Jack. She is going to bring him round tomorrow.

9th March

Disaster. I decided to go for a healthy tea. I was planning to talk to Natalie about making healthy eating choices anyway. She isn't fat – but she isn't slim either. She could go either way. Her mum and I always battled with our weight.

Natalie had told Jack that I did lovely teas. She was nearly in tears poor kid. I had really upset her and humiliated her in front of her new friend and I so did not mean to. She really likes this lad and wanted it to be just right. I'd gone for an organic chicken salad with croutons. Then fruit, crème freche, and some wholemeal oatie biscuits for pud. Thank God I had a raspberry pavlova in the freezer in case I had an emotional emergency myself. Well, I did. I'd upset Natalie and failed to impress a seriously hungry 15-year-old Jack. They divided it in half and sat squashed together on the sofa watching pre-school TV. It must be love.

I felt very foolish. I remember bringing a young man home for tea and being just as confused and embarrassed when I saw what a huge amount of trouble mother had gone to. Cups, saucers, cake stand and paper serviettes. I just wanted to show off what everyday life was like at home not special days.

I hope Natalie forgives me. I am so angry with myself.

10th March

I am now fully vegetarian.

I am thinking of becoming vegan.

12th March

I did NOT sleep last night.

I am having very dark thoughts.

I wonder if I should go and see Dr Janet. I think I could use something to help me sleep.

Dare I share my deepest thoughts? What if someone found this and read it?

13th March

BIG decision day.

If I don't share with you, dear Journal, who do I talk to?

Now I'm stumped.

Where to start...

23rd March

1.30am

Happy Birthday – to me.

I am having lunch with Geraldine – on her. I feel very flattered.

10pm

Bella has arrived.

Rob picked me up as planned for Birthday Cake and a drink round at theirs. Lovely surprise as Matt, Natalie and Alan were there. Also Jen's friend Alison. We had what Doreen described as a light supper of salad and salmon followed by a big trifle. I had a little and Doreen immediately leapt on me. She thought I should go to the doctor and get my own health checked out. I did my best not to rise – but there was an uncomfortable moment or two.

Then Rob and Matt brought this big box out with a ribbon tied round it. It was very obvious what it was because you could hear yelping and scratching – but I sort of played along for a moment saying how lovely the wrapping was and telling Doreen she should say pardon!

*Bella is conked out on her new bed by my feet. She is dreaming and making whimpering sounds. She has a hot water bottle by her in case she misses her mum and the other puppies. **<u>I do not need or want a dog.</u>** But the whole family seem to have been in on this and they really, really want to see me happy. I thought I was, but I have to admit maybe I haven't been feeling much recently apart from indignant and angry.*

Bella is a deep golden colour with fluffy ears.

I have been on line and found two vets in Brayston. I don't fancy Furry Friends Hospital and Surgery – it sounds Americanised to me and as though it's after your cash. I have settled on P. Humberstone and Partners. I will telephone G. in the morning and ask if she uses them for her cat. I can't see her as a Furry Friends sort of person. Bella will need her check and vaccinations.

For my birthday:

Bella from Doreen.

"Making the Impossible Happen: Eco-campaigning in the 21st century" by Adrian Peters from Geraldine.

A large fluffy, bright pink dog bed – not quite to my taste but I know Natalie chose it with great care – so it will be looked after as if it were alive.

A dog bowl with a bone pattern, red leather lead and collar from Matt.

A large stainless steel water bowl from Alan and a waterproof cover for the backseat of the car from Alison. Alison and Alan are 'an item' apparently.

Grooming brush, comb and some stuff to get stains up with from Rob.

Also cards from 2 neighbours, Beverley from school and Beryl, former colleague/friend.

I have spent the evening fussing over Bella and putting newspaper down all over the kitchen and hall. The slightest excitement and she wees. I know the problem. I have only let her explore the lounge, hall and kitchen. Doreen says it's important not to make the world too big for her to start with or get her over excited when you first bring her home. **_I don't honestly know what she's doing here._** *I can't really believe I agreed to bring her home. I keep looking down and wondering when Dor is coming to pick her up. Then I look again and think she looks so comfortable and she's not doing any harm.*

12.30am

Bella will not settle. I have shut her in the kitchen for the night and she is screaming the place down.

12.45am

i can't stand it any longer. i have brought her into the lounge and she is sitting on my lap as i write this with one finger. she is biting the fingers of my left hand. her teeth are as sharp as needles. she is eating as though food is going out of fashion. most of all she just seems to want a cuddle.

1.50am

Bella is asleep. She likes being sung to. She looks tiny in this huge cerise marshmallow thing of a bed. I sang to her "Little baby sweetly sleep" – took me back to when Jenny was a baby.

I am going to try and sleep.

4am

B. has peed on the bedroom carpet and I have a hole in my slipper.

10am

I have made up a chart. When Bella eats, goes out, has playtime and sits by me on a lead and not chewing. She has eaten part of the skirting board. She is teething. I will try a baby teething gel and see how she gets on with an ice cube.

24th March

Apart from having to get up at 4am. I slept the best I have in weeks. Bella must have woken and noticed I wasn't about so started crying. She will sleep on the bed. I know Dor says I should start as I mean to go on. Well I've started and I think I do mean to keep her now. Baby teething gel works a treat.

25th March

I have signed Bella on at Humberstone's and she is vaccinated.

Vet – Mr Humberstone described Bella as a "fine specimen". He said she was "bonnie" and was "as fit as a fiddle".

Toddy, Geraldine's cat is a regular there. Bella must not walk on pavements yet – so we are practising wearing a collar and lead in the garden. We managed a poo outside today. Bella, not me. She does make me laugh. I only have to call her once and she's off, waddling towards me. She seems so pleased to see me! Out of all proportion to the situation.

27th March

*I can't go on and on reading all this stuff on the internet and **not doing anything about it. There must be more I can do?***

Sometimes when a patient came in to see me and they were very anxious, worried that they had some terrible incurable disease or life was getting on top of them, I would encourage them to say what their worst fears were – get it outside their head and into the light as it were, so that they could see the thoughts for what they were – and decide what, if anything they wanted to do about them.

*I feel a bit like that now. I've got these thoughts, ideas, I suppose, running through my head and I want rid of them – or the courage to do something about them. I've racked my brains but I can't think of anyone I can talk to about this. People would think I was mad. The trouble is **I** don't think I am – and part of all these thoughts is the realisation that if my plan is to work, other people can't know. This is about me choosing to take control and do some thing that only I can do.*

I am fed up with Doreen telling me I am wasting away. I have started to add some layers of clothing and keep things loose-fitting. Look as though I am filling out again.

I am a bit worried that if I do write my ideas down it will look incriminating in some way. I've read in the paper about people having their computers investigated just because they are suspected of hitting on certain websites – and I don't mean the really bad ones – I mean just politically sensitive stuff.

Apparently they can even see things you've written in the heat of the moment and then deleted.

My first idea was to picket in the Worth It car park, as near the entrance as possible. I have found various websites with cheap secondhand caravans. I was going to sell the car. Get something that would pull a little caravan. Do a caravanning course for beginners – I am not clear how you back and manoeuvre with a caravan on the back – and then buy one. Bring it home. Measured the drive and it would be possible to park the caravan in front of the garage. I would have to park the car on the road, I think. I thought that if I practised and made up the stencils, I could probably spray paint something quite quickly onto the caravan's body work. I wouldn't want it sitting out on the drive for all to see for too long. Then I could take it to the supermarket car park and sit in. Hand out leaflets to anyone who will listen. I thought may be I could do a leaflet drop and put them on car windscreens.

Problems:

1. *Survival in the caravan in the car park could be an issue?? Even with help – Jelliebean and Geraldine would be up for it I am sure.*
2. *Could I leave the caravan – doubt it – someone might attempt to ransack it or tow it away?*
3. *Bella?*
4. *What are my rights in this??????*
5. *Will I be seen as a silly old woman?*
6. *Is this the best way to raise people's awareness? (It works for health issues).*

Bella is settling. She has discovered digging and flowerpots.

She will sit and lie down – just not for long.

1ˢᵗ April

Further thoughts.

What if I did a letter writing campaign – or tried to set up some sort of campaign with others? I have so far written twenty-three letters and received three replies. Maybe I should get more involved politically?

Slept for three hours I think last night.

3ʳᵈ April

BIG DAY.

Geraldine came to lunch HERE.

This was primarily to introduce her to Bella but also to say thank you to her. She has been very kind to me. She has been an inspiration and such an encouragement over the campaigning and thinking through what can, and cannot be done, realistically.

We had a tofu salad with lots of extra bits.

We then had fruits and a homemade meringue.

A dietary compromise.

Hopefully this helps you to understand a bit about how I came to do what I did, Matt and Natalie. It is hard to explain it simply - so I've included some notes from the days when I was on the road too. Nana

xx

Berrington Caravans and Dormobiles

New and second hand

17-19, Hazelworth Road, Flatford, West Midlands BR35 8DT

0120- 749-9043

www.berringtoncaravans.co.uk

Date: 12th April

Item

1 VW Campervan (1972) tax exempt £11,000

    Total:
 £11,000

    Including VAT

Cash paid

Received with thanks

Mrs Susan Graham
27, The Close,
Handbaston,
Wallhampton,
WA12 6HD

07776 385175

Could not be more content if I tried!!!!

<u>13th April</u>

I can't believe I've done it! She's a beauty! Turquoise blue and white! I have never carried or even seen so much cash as I held in my hand today. It was quite a thrill in a funny way. I was amazed how easy it was – turn up with cash and I knocked the guy down from £13,500 and she is in fantastic condition. No tax needed and she has really low mileage. Took it into a garage in Flatford to be checked over and they said it was as good as a museum piece – in a nice way – near perfect condition.

Amazed how easy it is to drive. Sold the mini easily enough on Online Auction would you believe.

Doreen was over yesterday, apparently the tom-tom's had informed her of my little purchase. She still thinks I'm joking when I say I want to go off and see the British Isles and take an extended painting holiday. Well I am – in a way – but she's not to know. Actually the more resistant she is to the idea the better I seem to be at sounding believable. Good practice. I can now say it without batting an eye-lid.

I have bought a crate for Bella – but so far she seems happy on the front seat in a little harness attached to the seat belt.

<u>15th April</u>

Bought a travel easel (£34) and a large canvas bag. I've ordered various art materials and watercolour pads on line. It's like Christmas when the postie rings the bell and I have another parcel to unwrap.

I have ordered a turquoise and white VW camper van key ring and a matching mug. I now need to choose the camper van's name!!!

Bella has learnt to bark – but not how to stop.

Itinerary

Drop One

Salisbury Worth It

Large car park

Xtra store

Wear wig and glasses

Large duffle coat

Hit: sausages

Return without wig but with glasses

Drop off doctored pack.

<u>Drive to Andover – overnight stay</u>

<u>Drive to Marlborough</u>

<u>2 days sketching</u>

Drop 2

Maximarket

On the A43

Large car park

Take Bella and tie up in entrance

Hit: Cornish pasties

Take Bella for walk.

Return doctored pack

Drive to just outside Oxford

Visit National Heritage house at Inglelington

Paint

Drop 3

Pearson's Hypermarket

on the A32

part of major retail park

Bob wig

Glasses

Thin coat

Hit: scotch eggs

Window shop

Set up package in van

Return package within the hour

Stay over in local caravan park at Hayley Woods.

- Well it's a start!!!

PROPOSED HITS:

~~*Salisbury*~~
~~*Marlborough*~~
~~*Abingdon*~~
~~*Swindon*~~
~~*Bath*~~
~~*Trowbridge*~~
~~*Yeovil*~~
~~*Axminster*~~
~~*Exmouth*~~
~~*Tenby*~~
~~*Swansea*~~
~~*Cardiff*~~
~~*Bangor*~~
~~*Blackpool*~~
~~*Leeds*~~
~~*York*~~
~~*Scarborough*~~
~~*Edinburgh*~~
~~*Inverness*~~
~~*Perth*~~
~~*Glasgow*~~
~~*Oban*~~
~~*Canterbury*~~
~~*Birmingham*~~

~~Beckingham~~

~~Tooting~~

~~Brighton~~

~~Ipswich~~

~~Folkestone~~

~~Cambridge~~

~~Bedford~~

~~Milton Keynes~~

~~Newport~~

~~Cardigan~~

~~St David's~~

~~Chester~~

~~Nottingham~~

~~Derby~~

~~Carlisle~~

~~Barnsley~~

~~Middlesborough~~

~~Ayr~~

Kendal

Hull

Lincoln

Worcester

Bristol

Stratford-upon-Avon

Canalside Cottage,
Chandler's Lane,
Wynleigh,
Brayston BY3 2PG

My Dear Babs,

I have taken longer than anticipated to reply because I was really, genuinely thunder-struck. Delighted; standing ovation; thrilled for you and for me.

I am so pleased you have embarked on the chemotherapy and radiotherapy. I could not be more certain that you are doing <u>the right thing</u>.

Yes, I am sure it is making you feel worse than "grotty", but this will not be how you feel forever. Hold on to that thought, my friend. Fantastic news about the scan. It is amazing what the power of positive thought can do.

I know you will smile and say I told you so, but I took the bull by the horns and went to see John Brown on my own account. I have had terrible problems with migraines and shoulder and neck pain. John is a terribly quiet and unassuming man. He examined me – with ALL my clothes on. Yes, I know we both wondered!!! He has worked on the shoulder, my neck and head for three sessions and I haven't had a migraine since! My shoulder very strangely hurt like pain was going out of fashion straight after the first session, but then I literally slept on it and in the morning it was fine – back to normal – pretty much.

Amazing. He doesn't actually touch you at all – his hands seem to hover over the area. I felt hot and cold – but it was actually very relaxing once I'd got over my initial uneasiness.

I am trying to hear what you are saying about not making a fuss on your release day – but you do need to have a heart. I, for one, would like to celebrate a very special day. I spoke briefly to Doreen this morning and we have agreed that I will come and pick you up. She would like to provide a light lunch (as requested) and I was planning to get some basic provisions ready in your bungalow. Maybe you would prefer to give me a list?

At the risk of repeating myself I would be thrilled if you came and stayed with me and allowed yourself some time to be pampered – just a little. It can't do you any harm!

On cloud nine!

With much love,

Gerladine   x

Canalside Cottage,
Chandler's Lane,
Wynleigh,
Brayston BY3 2PG

My Dear Babs,

I think you are right – I am so pleased to hear that you are wanting to take yourself seriously <u>and</u> that you are choosing to look after yourself. I have resisted doing anything much to the spare room as I thought it might be more comforting to arrive and settle in to a room which is pretty much as you will remember. I have changed sheets to organic and put in some of these new – and I find frightfully comfortable – memory pillows. I have set up with Steve the gardener's help a desk by the window and a couple of armchairs. There was a small TV in there anyway – and my one splash out was a clockwork digital radio!!

If anything else comes to mind that would make the transition easier, let me know. I wondered about getting you a new laptop, but decided this is a very personal choice.

In the meantime I am doing my best to practise not fussing.

Your friend, as always,

Geraldine

Grass Roots Community

14th May

Dear Natalie and Matt,

I wanted to tell you that whatever you feel about me as you read this file, I am still very proud and pleased to have known you.

Discovering I too had cancer was a devastating blow particularly as the tests came through when I was still on remand. The judge was compassionate and I had a short custodial sentence mainly because my prognosis was not looking good at the time. I would be lying if I didn't say that I was sure my time was up. If I am honest with you I think I longed to die. I felt very miserable a lot of the time.

The truth was that although I was of course content to plead guilty I was not in any real sense sorry for my part in the campaign. I was horrified and appalled by what followed, but the jury seemed to believe what was in fact the truth, that I had nothing to do with the horrible incidents where people put iron filings, broken glass and dog poo into food and returned it to Worth It. Looking back I guess I was naive. I thought a one woman campaign would be respected for what it was and allowed to run its course. I had allowed for some mistakes happening, but it honestly had not occurred to me that other people with, frankly, evil intent would get on the bandwagon. I saw myself as consciousness raising.

If I'd stopped and thought it through I should have realised. I will have to live with the knowledge that I really did mess up over that. In almost all campaigns which involve civil disobedience, at some point the weirdos and the psychopaths wade in and add their two penny worth. I should have realised that there was no reason why it would be different with this campaign.

My stay in hospital wasn't so bad. I was transferred to an open prison and I started my Open University degree. As far as I was concerned I had little time to live, but I decided to live as though I had all the time in the world - and try not to close my life down prematurely.

As you know I refused chemo and radiotherapy. I went to visualisation classes and when I was released I found the alternative healing for cancer centre in Markham Wood and I wasted no time in visiting them, really with the view of making my ending as gentle as possible. They insisted I take what options conventional medicine could offer. Gradually I saw their point. I had a choice to make - whether I really wanted to live or die.

I can't say they cured me - but the combination of an organic, vegan diet, gentle exercise, consciously reducing my stress levels combined with the healing sessions seemed to transform me from the inside out. I can't explain it, but my perspective changed. I no longer hated with a fearful anger. I wanted to love not hurt and I knew my loving needed to start with me. I have punished myself a lot over the years. For my two children that died, for my husband's death and for just not being good enough.

I don't know why I have been spared a short illness and a lingering death, but the tumour reduced in size and I remain in remission three years down the line.

Two and a half years longer than I was expected to live. There really hasn't been a magic cure. I have no doubt that at some point the cells will begin multiplying once again - and that will probably mean curtains, but for now my body seems to be holding up in what the healer at Markham Wood called a stasis. I understand it as staying at a point of equilibrium where for now, the cancer doesn't need to spread.

I discovered the Grass Roots Community through my addictive internet surfing. I needed a way of celebrating life. Grass Roots has provided me with a home and meaning - both spiritual and political. I went up incognito - old habits die hard! Had a look round and bought some gorgeous pottery in the shop. I suspected they may be a lot of ageing hippies with too much time on their hands. Some of them are - but the place felt real and actually quite ordinary. I spent ages in the café just people watching and reading a book I'd bought in the second hand bookshop. I was relieved I wasn't the only one - there was a man in his mid sixties, I would guess with a long white beard and a ponytail who was typing away on his laptop as though his life depended on it. I was pleased to see that the café had wifi!

I looked round the area in my little rented Ka. It is such a beautiful part of the world. Stunning scenery and the people seem so warm and caring. It was refreshing.

I went home determined to find out more.

I know your Dad has wanted me out of your lives for a long time - and I do know he has lied to you about my circumstances. Now that you have come of age, Natalie, it is time for you to make your own mind up about your Gran. I do not condone what your Dad did. I do not think it is ever a good idea to lie to children, but I have to give him the benefit of the doubt because he is your father.

I know it will be a big shock to know I am still alive. I hope the attached helps you understand what is important to me now - and it will help you find me if you ever decide you want to be in touch again. I hope it will also help you to understand why I now know life is so entirely intended to be lived - and I am living.

I hope the attached will also help you to understand how I have come to be me.

With love,

Barbara.

Grass Roots Community Village,
Organic Smallholding
And Craft Centre
Andlescombe
By Murdo
Nr Inverness
IV7 5KG

www.grassrootscommunity.org

Grass Roots is a residential community based in Inverness-shire, in the Highlands of Scotland. Located on the shore of the Merne Firth. It evolved over many years as the result of the vision of Hamish and Sally Arbroath, two mystical healers and educationalists based in the area.

Hamish and Sally Arbroath

Founders of Grass Roots

Hamish, a keen horticulturalist and artist began to experiment with meditation and plant growth, quickly tapping into the deep resources of Mother Earth, Sister Gaia as a means of enhancing plant well-being and maintaining healthy, happy crops.

Sally, a former musician and teacher, spotted the potential to create a community that would offer an alternative to the highly consumerist and resource ravaging lifestyles that so many indulge in today. After gathering "The Pilgrims", a group of ecologically minded companions, they began their search for a smallholding to realise their dream. Sally has departed this life, but she has left a number of meditations which are used by members of the community and friends of the community to this day.

Where are we?

The former RAF base had been something of a blot on the Inverness-shire landscape for many years. After much negotiation it was bought by Hamish and Sally with a family bequest. Over the last thirty years, Grass Roots claimed a unique life on this base and is now a thriving home for community members, visitors and friends of the charitable foundation.

Places to visit in our community settlement:

Grass Roots Little Big Farm

Within the 10 acre site we have a smallholding dedicated to rare breed pigs and sheep, as well as growing in poly tunnels a wide variety of organic produce. On the Merne Firth you will also see an impressive variety of water fowl, including over-wintering geese and the extremely rare Rustle Duck.

Grass Roots Farm Shop

Is open Monday through to Saturday from 10am - 5pm. We have a small bakery attached. We produce homemade and locally resourced bread, cheeses, milk, eggs, meat and vegetables. We also stock a wide range of dried goods and drinks which are Fairly traded.

Grass Roots Gallery

Is run by Deidre Valentine. It provides an exhibition space for local artists and craftspeople from within the community. All items on show are available for purchase. The Gallery stocks paintings, sculpture, ceramics and jewellery.

In addition there is a vintage clothes section and a Swop It shop where second-hand items can be swopped or purchased.

All items are based on a fundamental principle of recycling.

The Gaia Meditation and Healing Space

Is used on a daily basis for meditation, mindfulness and acts of worship and synchronicity. We have daily Healing sessions at 5pm.

Rav Pendip and Sheila Wallace co-ordinate the Centre.

The Cosmos Auditorium

Is a specially created hay bale build with sedum roof circular structure. This space offers a major conference or teaching space. It is used for large meetings, dance, music and major exhibitions.

Molly's

Molly's is a small café which is open from 10-4pm every day. There is a variety of snacks, cakes and drinks on sale as well as a small second-hand bookshop.

Homemade candles, polished stones from the shore and freshly cut flowers (when in season) are also sold here. Wifi.

Grass Roots Art Space

The Art Space is fully equipped with a variety of materials, easels and computer equipment.

Workshops and play days are advertised on our website.

Grass Roots Library and Resource Centre

Although the Resource Centre is open to the public, the library is for community members only.

Grass Roots Garden of Remembrance

Is situated on the shore and is a place where ashes can be scattered or interred.

Sticky Fingers and The Layabouts Recreation Space

Adapted for children and young people, this space is open each afternoon between 3.30pm and 6pm and on Sunday evenings from 6-9pm.

Community Accommodation

The base community are permanent members of the Grass Roots Community and live there all the year round. Each household has a converted hut, new build eco-build or a section of an aircraft hangar which has been fitted out as unusual, but ecologically sound living units. People stay at the community for anything up to a year and reside in static caravans. Those shorter term visitors stay either in our camping field which has toilets, showers and a utility room, or in our singles hut.

Sustainability and Health Campaign

Jelliebean, Geralddream and Bulgebattler (their internet handles – check them out on *PeopleDirect*) – our three virtual and actual eco-warriors –

mastermind and initiate a number of national and international campaigns to encourage sustainability and a critical reassessment of how our limited resources are successfully stewarded.

www.grassrootssustainability.org

Campaigns include:

Food messenger – late noughties and early tens.

Dumper trucking ministers

e-campaign to change the 2011 Food Management Act

Fair trade

Recycling packaging

Small business rights

Outing food wasters

DEATH to Additives; additive is death campaign

Children for good food trust

Processing kills advertisements in the national press

4, The Birches,
Brayston,
BY1 4DC.

Mr Hamish Arbroath,
The Grass Roots Community,
Andlescombe,
Nr Murdo,
Inverness-shire,
IV7 5KG.

Dear Mr Arbroath,

    I have recently found The Grass Roots Community website and notice that you are in a position to consider applications to join the community.

    I would appreciate it if you could send me details of how I apply as I am very interested in doing so.

    I look forward to hearing from you.

    Yours sincerely

Barbara Drapper

Barbara Drapper

Canalside Cottage,
Chandler's Lane,
Wynleigh,
Brayston
BY3 2PG

Mr Hamish Arbroath,
The Grass Roots Community,
Andlescombe,
Nr. Murdo,
Inverness-shire,
IV7 5KG

Dear Mr Arbroath,

A very dear friend of mine, Barbara Drapper, has shared with me all the details she has found of The Grass Roots Community on the world wide web. We have in recent years campaigned together over sustainability issues. I am writing to enquire further, as I know Barbara is too, about how I might apply for a place in your community. I visited your community a month ago with Barbara during a short visit to the Highlands. I was very struck by the ethos and the work you undertake.

You do not mention an age limit in your general details, however, to avoid wasting your time, and possibly mine, I feel I should state from the outset that I am 70 years of age. Although hale and hearty I am obviously not as young or as strong as you may wish, however I bring with me a lifetime of skills and a passion for all things ecological.

I very much look forward to hearing from you in due course.

With warmest good wishes,

Yours sincerely,

Geraldine Walton

Email: Geralddreama@hotmail.co.uk

Grass Roots Community
Andlescombe, By Murdo
Inverness-shire
IV7 5KG

01463 753753

www.grasrootscommunity.org

email: Hamish@grassrootscommunity.org

Dear Barbara,

Thank you for your letter. I have enclosed with my letter a copy of our current person specification. We try very hard not to be too prescriptive and we welcome people whose skills and gifts will complement or contrast with existing community member portfolios.

We maintain equality of opportunity and have no age restrictions. In the case of a person applying who has previously existing serious medical conditions, we require a medical prior to the confirmation of their place in community. This is with a view to offering appropriate support, if required.

Namaste.

Yours sincerely,

Hamish

Grass Roots Community

Person Specification For Community Members

Essential Attributes:

- Evidenced commitment to sustainability.
- Evidenced commitment to and understanding of community living.
- Already leading a committed life based on sustainability and recycling good practice.
- In reasonable physical and mental good health.
- Good sense of humour.
- Willingness to engage with others on a wide variety of levels.
- A spiritual life of some kind.
- A capacity to enjoy your own company and space.
- A skill or experience that will enhance the existing communal life.

Desirable Attributes:

- IT skills.
- DIY, maintenance, smallholding or crafting skills.

- Cooking skills.
- Commitment to pledge hours to the maintenance of a healthy community.
- Meditation, healing, worship or other spiritual skills.
- Chairing, minute taking, administration.
- Musical and/or drama skills

Applications via a letter of application and two referees.

Why do I want to be in community?

The community/2/10/jobdes/ipeg

4, The Birches,
Brayston,
BY1 4DC.

Mr Hamish Arbroath,
The Grass Roots Community,
Andlescombe,
By Murdo,
Inverness-shire,
IV7 5KG.

Dear Mr Arbroath,

Thank you for your letter.

I found the person specification very helpful and it has certainly given me food for thought.

What I need to say first of all is that I do come with some fairly alarming (to some people) baggage. I wouldn't describe myself as screwed up or cynical or long in the tooth, but other people have accused me of being one of these, if not all three!

I have enclosed with this letter my psychiatric report and a not untypical press report. You haven't mentioned any rules and regulations about taking people into the community who have a history of mental health problems. You haven't said that you do not take people who have a criminal record either. I therefore thought it would be best if I wrote and told you about these two things before I spent time working on an application letter.

I spent a year in prison. I contravened my probation order. I had already been found guilty of starting a food campaign which drew attention to the carcinogenic qualities of most additives and preservatives, not to mention the difficulties trans fats cause our cardio-vascular system.

My original plan was to put rice paper messages in foods and return them to the store I had purchased them from. Sadly a young woman was badly shocked and injured in this campaign. I gave myself up and was given twelve months probation. At that time I undertook a full psychiatric assessment and was diagnosed with bowel cancer. I am, very fortunately, now in remission. I was diagnosed with severe depression. I now take antidepressants.

When I was on probation I continued to operate as a food activist and increased the intensity of the campaign by adding food dye and washing up liquid to meat products. At no time did I add more dangerous products to foods. This part of the campaign was undertaken by another activist. I have no idea who.

In addition, I do want to stress that I am not homosexual and that Geraldine Walton is not my partner in any way shape or form. I was married for 35 years before my husband died. I have a daughter – who died three years ago. I am not homophobic either.

I am sure you understand that the above information is sensitive, but I felt I would be being less than honest, if I did not tell you about this before we went any further.

I look forward to hearing from you.

Yours sincerely,

Barbara Drapper

Mrs B. Drapper

Defender

Global

Read today's paper – Jobs Search

Defender Global The Defender

Home   UK   Audio   World News   Now
   Blogs   Search   Arts   Media

BRAYSTON WOMAN PLEADS GUILTY TO SUPERMARKET REIGN OF TERROR

Jodie Ammerton

Monday November 29th

The Defender

Barbara Drapper, 64, has pleaded guilty at Wellingbridge Crown Court to causing 12 counts of actual bodily harm. Drapper, a widow, was on probation following a previous incident of food tampering when she was caught red-handed inflicting her gruesome punishments on unsuspecting members of the general public.

Drapper, a trained nurse, had already been given a 12 month suspended sentence for administering poisonous and noxious things, when she was brought in for questioning following another nationwide supermarket campaign of horror. Shoppers were becoming increasingly fearful for their families and their own personal safety as they attempted to check food packaging to see if it had been tampered with prior to purchase. Across the nation cautious shoppers could be seen unwrapping refrigerated goods and leaving them on the counter if they had any doubts about their freshness. In supermarkets and grocery outlets terror was mounting as random items continued to be found containing messages of doom referring to additives and preservatives.

Drapper, along with her partner Geraldine Walton, 68, had been known to the security at the *Worth It* food empire for some months. Initially they were brought to the attention of security in their local Brayston store as they joined many women campaigners in the Women's Federation Packaging Campaign.

Drapper, described by the Chairman of *Worth It* Sir Bradley Winterton as "a psychopath and mad food terrorist", who couldn't resist taking her campaign message a stage further in the summer of last year, began her reign of terror travelling through the British countryside dropping off doctored packets of meat products at *Worth It* stores. With a mind warped by her belief that everyday foods have the power to bring about our early death, she coolly planned a campaign whilst on remand, which would make her a figure of eco-campaigning legend and an icon of fear to supermarket magnates. She believed the public weren't responding quickly enough to her crazy pleas and so she upped the ante, delivering packs of meat products with washing-up liquid, green food dye, iron filings and ground glass mashed into them. Police Inspector Greenlowe states that Drapper's campaign did not include filings and glass, and confirms that he has taken her case to the Crown Prosecution Service, in other words "Drapper's game is up".

Judge Downley, in his summing up of this dastardly, disturbed woman and her feckless campaign, stated that he would make an example of her to all would be eco terrorists, making sure they realised, once and for all, that such behaviours could not, and would not, be acceptable in civilised society.

Drapper, as one of her victims, Bob Shaw, commented "got off lightly". Diagnosed with terminal cancer she will serve just six months of a three year sentence.

Geraldine Walton, who was not charged following the police investigation, refused to comment as she left court. Her neighbour, Mrs Annabel Hamilton-Greyes, 63, said how shocked she was by the whole episode. "One does not expect one's neighbours to act in such a cavalier fashion in this day and age. Miss Walton was considered an upright member of the local community; a former Headmistress of a girls' public school. One cannot even begin to imagine whatever possessed her. Now had it been the campaign to save the local hunt, she would have garnered significant sympathy, understanding and local support."

Drapper is being held at HMP Starling and is expected to transfer to an open prison within the next week.

Grass Roots Community
Andlescombe, By Murdo
Inverness-shire
IV7 5KG

01463 753753

www.grassrootscommunity.org

email: Hamish@grassrootscommunity.co.uk

Dear Barbara,

Thank you for your honest and informative letter.

I took the liberty of making some enquiries through our own team who work on our Sustainability and Health Projects. I discussed your food campaign in very general terms with the Project's Co-ordinator, Jeremy, without any reference to your letter. You will, I am sure, be delighted to read that Jeremy talked not only very warmly about you but with great authority and enthusiasm about your campaigning strategies. He said that at one time he had "the privilege" of being in email contact with you and talked about how you and he had shared a certain disgust over supermarket packaging. You may recall him by his on-line handle, Jelliebean.

Jeremy was able to provide me with considerable evidence of just how effective your campaign had actually been.

As far as I am concerned I can see no problem in moving to the formal stage of a letter of application as long as you are prepared for me to disclose to the group, who consider all applications, our previous correspondence. There would be no need for you to mention any of our previous correspondence in your letter of application unless you feel it is necessary.

With all good wishes as you discern your future,

Yours sincerely,

Hamish

4, The Birches,
Brayston,
BY1 4DC.

Mr Hamish Arbroath,
The Grass Roots Community,
Andlescombe,
By Murdo,
Inverness-shire,
IV7 5KG.

Dear Hamish,

Thank you for your reassuring letter. Further to your comments, I am writing this as a letter of application.

I read and thought a lot about your person specification. I wouldn't be me if I didn't initially think I'm not sure I can do this, but I realise this is a discernment process for you as well as me.

Although I am embarrassed and in turn ashamed by my record in sustainability, it is fair to say that I do have a reputation for and a record of direct action. I have often looked back at what I did and wondered if I did do the right thing. Could I have found a better way of taking action which didn't involve any chance of hurting innocent by-standers?

The awful truth is that the gentler campaign run by the Women's Federation attracted the news and media coverage for days, maybe a month or two. It encouraged low level local action, but in reality very little changed in the marketing practices of the major supermarket chains. The "Say no to processed food" has saved lives and has challenged how the supermarkets feed us. We now have legislation entering its final reading which will prohibit the use of the worst additive and preservative offenders.

Would I do it again? Possibly not. Possibly. The cost to my family, friends and even myself has been great.

I have never lived in community, beyond the smallest community of my family. It appeals to me, but I am very apprehensive. I hope I am still flexible, but I suspect I may not be. I am committed to trying and to giving it my very best shot. I think, for me, the biggest challenge will be in understanding what privacy means in a communal setting. In some ways I am a very private person, but I do know I am also quite caring and hard working.

The nearest I have got to communal living is working in a hectic medical centre as a practice nurse. Within my role I was well used to supporting a very wide variety of people and generally I found I not only enjoyed this, but was successful in this role.

I have discussed with you in a previous letter my physical and mental health. I do give you permission to share the content of that letter with the selection group.

I think I have a reasonably good sense of humour.

I have a dog – always a good sign and a camper van called Rocinante – which counts for something!

I have a great concern for the well being of our planet and for all creation, but I would not describe myself as a religious person. I am comfortable around people who are religious.

I've thought a lot about what sorts of skills I might bring to community. I would be really interested in supporting the work of the sustainability and health project. I have kept pretty up to date with medical developments and feel I still have something constructive to add to sustainability campaigning. I don't have a particular desire to be an activist, but I would enjoy working to support others who take direct action behind the scenes.

Practically, I am a keen computer user. I enjoy painting in watercolour and drawing in pastels, although I have never sold my work. I am a keen flower and vegetable gardener. I have grade IV piano. I can play simple tunes, but I don't currently practise regularly. When I was working in the medical practice I chaired the ancillary staff's committee and I had responsibility for inducting all new staff.

What I would bring to community is easier to answer if I think about what I hope to get out of the experience. I want to learn more about sustainability and I want to help. To feel I was useful would make me feel as though I belong. I would love having people to care about too and I know that when I care for people there is a chance they might care back.

I hope this helps you as you consider my application.

If you have any other questions please do not hesitate to contact me.

Yours sincerely,

Barbara Drapper

Barbara Drapper (Mrs)

Grass Roots Community
Andlescombe, By Murdo
Inverness-shire
IV7 5KG

01463 753753

www.grassrootscommunity.org

email: Hamish@grassrootscommunity.co.uk

Dear Barbara,

Thank you so much for your letter of application. I am delighted to tell you that we have considered your letter and we would very much like to proceed to the next stage and invite you to come and stay with the community for a week of discernment.

I have included with this letter our booklet "A Guide to those discerning community life" which we hope will be of help to you as you prepare for your visit.

We look forward to hearing from you which week you would like to come. We are very happy to pick you up from the train station and ferry you to Grass Roots.

We very much look forward to meeting you in person. If you have any other questions in the interim, please do not hesitate to give me a ring or email me.

With best wishes,

Yours sincerely,

Hamish

Grass Roots Community
Andlescombe, By Murdo
Inverness-shire
IV7 5KG

01463 753753

www.grassrootscommunity.org

email: Hamish@grassrootscommunity.co.uk

Dear Barbara,

It was a pleasure to meet you. I am hoping that this letter will be waiting for you on your return home. The selection group have met for meditation and discussion and were unanimous that we wished to proceed to the next stage of discernment.

Referring to the Grass Roots guide which you received with your original application, the next stage in the process is for you to come and spend a minimum of a month with us living and experiencing working as a member of the community. At the end of that time, you will be invited to consider with me, and with the selections group, what your future holds in terms of the Grass Roots Community.

If you would be kind enough to let me know whether in the first instance, you wish to undertake this next stage, and in the second if/when you might wish to come, I can make arrangements accordingly.

With warmest good wishes for your discernment,

Yours,

Hamish

4, The Birches,
Brayston,
BY1 4DC.

Mr Hamish Arbroath,
The Grass Roots Community,
Andlescombe,
By Murdo,
Inverness-shire,
IV7 5KG.

Dear Hamish,

Thank you so much for your swift response. It was a real pleasure to get your letter on my return.

I was very relieved that you do want to see me again and I am very pleased to write that I would like to accept your invitation.

I would like to come and stay from 1st March if this is convenient to you and the community.

I look forward to hearing from you.

With all good wishes,

Barbara

Grass Roots Community

Andlescombe, By Murdo
Inverness-shire
IV7 5KG

01463 753753

www.grassrootscommunity.org

email: Hamish@grassrootscommunity.co.uk

Dear Barbara,

Thank you for your decisive letter. The community join me in saying that we are all very much looking forward to your extended stay with us.

I believe that Amelia showed you round our available single person's accommodation on site. She tells me as our Welcomer that the Biggs room – named after the author not the train robber – would be available for March. It has such a pleasant aspect with the sea view. You will recall it is a self-contained unit with sitting room, kitchen, shower room and bedroom. We provide a starter pack of basic foods and household stuffs – so please don't overload yourself on your journey.

You will need to bring your own bed linen, duvet, pillows, towels and tea towels.

If you are travelling by train, we will meet you at Inverness station if you telephone or email us with your arrival time. If you are travelling by car, we encourage you to make your way to my home – on the left of the folly as you arrive – or to the office if you arrive in office hours and we will see you settled in.

Namaste,

Hamish

4, The Birches,
Brayston,
BY1 4DC.

Mr Hamish Arbroath,
The Grass Roots Community,
Andlescombe,
By Murdo,
Inverness-shire,
IV7 5KG.

Dear Hamish,

You asked me to get home after my stay, put my feet up and give myself plenty of time before I made up my mind as to whether or not I wanted to accept your invitation to become a permanent member of the community.

I think you have got to know me well enough in the last weeks to guess that I am actually writing this sitting in a service station having enjoyed a remarkably good vegetarian curry, and as I look out over a pond full of fish and ducks! I am sure my tea will get cold, but who cares!

I feel like a child who has had to go home after a fantastic birthday party. I was very reluctant to leave. I am not a naturally impetuous person, but I think I can say with certainty that the last time I felt this confident about a decision I accepted my husband's proposal of marriage!

Before I say much more in my haste, I want to thank you and the team – especially Betty and Deidre for their good humour and patience. Also Jeremy and you, of course!!! I had a really good time at Grass Roots, although it was not without its hiccoughs. I think I learnt a lot about myself while I was with you and I am ashamed to admit that I didn't know myself at all well before.

I can't hold it in any more – but with my heart and mind and my soul (still not sure quite where this begins and ends!) I would like to say yes to your invitation. I have not felt so at home or appreciated in years.

As I say I don't think I am looking at Grass Roots through rose coloured spectacles. It's much harder work than I ever imagined. I don't mean the twelve hours a week working with Jerry on the project – that was a pleasure – more the day to day stuff. I've not been sure before that I liked people that much – I've come away from Grass Roots realising that the person I haven't liked much is actually me. It is tough rubbing alongside such a variety of people each day and I find it hard work to try and just be myself and not get overly involved.

I did find some people difficult and there were a few nights I can tell you when I burnt the midnight oil worrying about what I could do to improve the situation. I found the talks we had very helpful as they helped me gain some sort of perspective. I think you are right that I do need to learn not to take so much to heart. I don't think I expected people to be quite so normal, I thought they'd all be a bit needy and neurotic. Yes, I know I am judgemental – and in my judgement there probably are some like that – but I can also see how we all fit together with all our own little ways – and somehow after a lot of forgiving, forgetting and silence – we muddle along.

If I have a fear it is that I will die before I have a chance to really fully enjoy the Grass Roots experience. There's no rational reason for this. So I must live with my new hope and energy.

I loved the Biggs Room and Amelia has said (I hope this is right) that for the agreed rent and community contribution I could return and take up permanent residence in it. I would very much like to do this although I could make a home in one of the single rooms if this is difficult.

As we have discussed I am in a very fluid place at the moment. My home has been made over to my grandchildren and they will become the legal owners when they are both over 21. In the meantime it is my intention to rent the property out. I have relatively little to clear out as I did quite a lot of laying the past to rest before I went on my "rampage" trying to save the planet!

I will need a couple of months to have the bungalow decorated throughout and some fresh carpets put down ready for the let. I can pack most of what I need in my trusty camper van – and anything I can't I can find a haulage firm to transport.

I feel so excited. I can't tell you.

As things stand I would anticipate travelling north – or should I say travelling home? on or around the 1st June. Summer in the highlands! Yes, I know you have told me to get a thicker overcoat!

Do, please, tell Amelia that there really is nothing I need doing in Biggs. It is wonderful.

Hamish, thank <u>you</u> so much for all the time you gave to me as I was trying to work out what was troubling me. You have really helped me to clear my head and look forward instead of back. I will be indebted to you for the rest of my life for that.

I will have to break it to Bella gently that she has a new home!!!!

With love,

Barbara x

Grass Roots Community
Andlescombe, By Murdo
Inverness-shire
IV7 5KG

01463 753753

www.grassrootscommunity.org

email: Hamish@grassrootscommunity.co.uk

Dear Barbara,

It was a delight to receive your enthusiastic letter full of such kind words. Thank you. We are all delighted by your decision. I shared the highlights of your letter at this week's community meal and you received a loud round of applause and Jerry whistled! I think I can safely say people are very much looking forward to welcoming you on June 1st. If by any chance your plans do change, please, do contact me via e-mail or phone.

Amelia tells me that she would like to re-tile the shower room before you come simply because some of the tiles are cracked. She is very happy to be advised by you regarding colour etc... I think she has seen a recycled pebbles motif she likes but you can contact her and discuss this further via

Daintypants@grassrootscommunity.org.

Can I add my personal congratulations to those of the community. On a personal note, I enjoyed the talks we had enormously and I felt you brought perspective to my thinking too – particularly over the reed bed saga!

I very much look forward to welcoming you into community.

With warmest good wishes,

Hamish

Brayston

Dear Hamish,

Your letter was a great encouragement, arriving as it did just as I was beginning to despair. I have badly over-estimated just how much I want to bring north and I am beginning to feel as though I might as well just chuck it all out and be done with it! Do I really <u>need</u> all these things?

I think my biggest problem is with photo albums, records and CDs, old paintings and tools. I think the gardening tools can find a home in the farm tool shed – can you have too many spades, mowers etc??? I didn't realise just how many photo albums and boxes of photos I had. What do I do with <u>them?</u> The natural place would be the grandchildren but that option isn't open to me. I have tried to weed out the non-essential photos but it takes hours, I am so slow – and then there are gaps and I spend another hour or more trying to find another photo of a similar vintage that I want to keep. I can hear you saying that I am being Little Miss Perfect – but old habits die hard.

I am wondering now whether to hire a man with a van to come up with all my bits and bobs. Unless I've suddenly imagined Biggs is an awful lot bigger than I remember I think I am right in thinking I can fit my stuff in and then sort things out gradually – maybe even donate for the shop etc… does that sound possible?

I am trying very hard not to get into a long round of goodbyes and farewells. I think all my energy is going on the move and if I am honest, I think in my heart I am already there with you all.

Lots of love,

Babs

Grass Roots Community
Andlescombe, By Murdo
Inverness-shire
IV7 5KG

01463 753753

www.grassrootscommunity.org

email: Hamish@grassrootscommunity.co.uk

Dear Barbara,

A joy to receive your letter. You obviously are up to your eyes in the move. Do try and go as gently as you can. I do know what it is like trying to finally sort out what you actually need for the rest of the journey.

You do not need my permission to bring your belongings into your new home. It's entirely your own affair if you want to pack it from floor to ceiling with boxes – not that I am anticipating from your letter that this is actually your intention.

I am sure Dougal will be thrilled to welcome new tools into his store and the shop is always grateful for donations. It never surprises me that it is absolutely true that one person's rubbish is another person's treasure!

You mentioned that you were thinking you might employ a man with a van. At the risk of imposing on you, I would be more than happy to travel down with the Grass Roots van. I can bring a sleeping bag etc... as I would guess by then you will be all packed up and raring to go! It really would be enjoyable for me. I like driving and I can take a scenic route on the way down at least – not so justifiable with a heavy load on board.

Let me know if this would be acceptable to you, it would be my pleasure.

With best regards for your packing and preparations,

Hamish

Brayston

Dear Hamish,

I can't believe you really mean it? This is <u>so</u> kind of you. If you really don't mind I would be thrilled if you could be my man with a van!

You are, of course, right, by the time you come I will have sold the beds and there will be very little still out apart from the wok and the kettle. I'm sure we'll manage. I was planning to drive Rocinante up to Inverness with one load and then after a few days' rest, go back down and get another – so this will speed things up unbelievably. We could drive up at our own speeds and maybe meet en route for a meal somewhere? My treat. I would also like to pay for the van and your time if that's OK?

I do know in my head that I don't need to ask permission to do things in community, but it does still feel a little bit like going off to a select boarding school for grown ups and I think it will take me a little while to realise the reality of what I know you are anxious that I take on board.

I found your comment about deciding what I need for the rest of my own personal journey a really helpful yardstick when I look at my possessions and decide what to take. I am amazed at how little I need. The memories are important but it's things like my CDs and paints that will feed me now and in the future.

Time to live now.

With love and gratitude,

Babs

BBC Radio Transcript
"Decision Time"
Broadcast:
Tuesday 16th January
9.30am, 9.30pm and 1.10am

Presenter: Mr Michael Clott
Contributor: Mrs Barbara Drapper
Researcher: Claudia Eggerly
Producer: Thor Vendrickssen

Michael: Welcome to "Decision Time".

Barbara Dapper is a retired medical practice nurse originally from the market town of Brayston, in the sleepy West Country's rolling hills. Barbara led an exemplary life serving her community through her chosen vocation and by managing a busy home and raising a daughter. To all intents and purposes, Barbara was typical of her background and training; law abiding and conscientious until her husband died suddenly from a heart attack. Within a matter of months, her daughter was diagnosed with breast cancer and died. By then Barbara was suffering from depression. She decided it was time to take the law into her own hands. Angry and disassociated by her recent bereavements, she became convinced that additives, preservatives and pesticides affect the quality of life. Barbara began a campaign of civil disobedience – tampering with foodstuffs on supermarket shelves by adding sinister doom-laden warnings. Her campaign was largely ignored in the national press and so she increased the intensity of her campaign by using more damaging substances mixed with food. The media became hysterical as her campaign gained momentum, blaming everyone from terrorists to the supermarkets themselves allegedly hungry for publicity, however adverse. Barbara was eventually captured, brought to justice and served a prison sentence. Barbara then discovered she too had cancer and experienced what remains little short of a miracle, her cancer ceased spreading. She now lives in remission, which, as she says herself, was unexpected by everyone. Along the way, as Barbara campaigned, two government ministers have been sacked; an election was won or lost on attitudes to issues of food health; a raft of preventative legislation made its progress through Parliament; and a number of subsequent campaigns literally took root and blossomed through Barbara's on-going work with The Grass Roots Community in Inverness-shire.

Barbara, you went to an enormous amount of trouble to bring this issue to the attention of the general public, why didn't you just keep quiet, remain a model citizen and concentrate on altering your own diet and those of your family?

Barbara: Well I did change my diet as much as I could, but I soon discovered my food choices were very limited by what was actually available, particularly through the supermarkets.

You know I think that taking the action I did means I am actually a model citizen – engaged in society and not frightened to blow the whistle.

When I first got interested in food, I was pretty unaware of the effect it could have on healthy living and life expectancy. My main concern really was to lose weight. I did a lot of research on the web and made a huge number of notes. I can't tell you the hours I spent in the supermarkets just looking at the contents of various foods – even those that looked fresh and untarnished. I became very aware pretty quickly that there was a causal link between the various preservatives and additives, not to mention pesticides that were in use and the various illnesses that dominate Western society – cancer and cardio-vascular in particular. Why are contents still in such tiny writing, by the way?

Sodium Nitrate is a good example. It's used for colouring and flavouring, to increase shelf life. You used to find large quantities of it in processed meats and cheese. It's still around. It's an ominous substance. Sodium Nitrate converts haemoglobin into another substance in the blood which is not nearly as effective at carrying oxygen round in our blood supply. Having a large burger and fries before a major amount of exercise could be dangerous. Very dangerous indeed. Our bodies need a regular supply of oxygen to survive. Simple as.

I realised too that all these chemicals are now present in the food chain and assimilated into the earth. We are not just killing ourselves, but killing our planet too. Just on a human level, it didn't seem possible to me that so many people could be dying from cancer without there being some environmental cause or contributory factor. I found and exposed one significant cause. I couldn't just sit on my hands and pretend I hadn't discovered all this.

Michael: There had been many DEFRA led investigations that indicate that the link between pesticides and terminal illness is negligible.

Barbara: But it isn't; figures can be massaged. There are a higher percentage of people who work or have worked with pesticides who are sterile, have had children with deformities, or who have developed cancer. DEFRA know this. They also know that if they were to release undoctored figures, the general public would be up in arms and want an explanation as to why they have been treated in this way.

Michael: You genuinely think that this is a matter best dealt with through civil disobedience?

Barbara: I genuinely think it is. Anything which is too sensible or too reasoned, people stop and think for a minute and then dismiss what they've heard. We all have a bit of "Well, it will never happen to me" in us. Sometimes extreme behaviour is the only way to encourage people to stop and take serious note. Stop and ask – why is someone putting their own neck on the line like this, if it really is nothing? We now have the legislation through. Britain's nutrition was in a very, very different place ten years ago. We'd only just begun to cotton on to the key issues about saving the planet. We were in denial as a nation about the effect processed foods were having. We were even behind the United States, which is saying something. We wouldn't have achieved what we have if some people hadn't seen that things needed to change radically and fast.

Michael: Surely even matters of ecology are ultimately about personal choice?

Barbara: Not really. You see back then, the options were so limited. People were very slowly waking up to a world that was unsustainable. They were only just beginning to think the unthinkable and realise that the consequences for the planet were disastrous. I was no different from anyone else. I thought it was enough to buy fairly traded goods and recycle. My mind was gradually changed when I became more actively involved in civil disobedience.

Let's face it, we were contemplating a world which felt as though it was going back in time. We were being asked to consider power cuts to sustain resources; to think of alternative ways to heat our homes; we were aware that we were using up the planet's resources at three times the rate she could sustain and it looked as though the only way to stop ourselves killing the earth was to cut back big time. Maybe return literally to the dark ages. We had got used to a way of living which meant everything was literally on a plate whether it was cheap, sweetened and highly processed food, or the latest gadgets and gizmos. We had lost the knack of cooking and eating well; mending and making do – even saving before we buy. As an individual you can choose to try and live differently but in reality everything was stacked against freedom of choice. I can remember wanting to buy some flag stones for the fireplace one summer. My husband and I thought we'd like some local stone. We went to the suppliers. A couple of local slabs were three times the price of the reconstituted stone that looked much the same, and was manufactured in China. Madness.

Michael: Was civil disobedience ever an appropriate course of action?

Barbara: Yes, I think it was. There had been a number of ecological campaigns that were mildly disobedient like the Women's Federation and the Earth Campaigners stuff; but they were primarily concerned with smallish, single issue concerns. In their own way they were highly effective. The more shoppers who removed packaging at the point of purchase, the more the large supermarket chains were forced to reconsider their packaging policy. With the Copenhagen Ecological Agreement sustainability became a very live issue internationally. It was the beginning of the saving of the planet. Meanwhile at a commercial level, supermarket policies were responding to the issues shoppers were raising. You would hardly know now when you shop in your average supermarket, but packaging was a serious issue in the nineties. Just as in the nineties there were plastic bags handed out with shopping – now we would just laugh with complete disbelief at the wastage and inappropriateness of it all.

There was a point when it was impossible to conceive of any other option. It became necessary because the cause became urgent – earth threatening – the protection of human life – and there were no other quick solutions.

Michael: So what tipped you over the edge?

Barbara: I became aware quite suddenly of the extent of the problem. The additions in food were a silent and pervasive killer of all I held dear. Writing a few letters didn't seem nearly enough, I learnt that early on in my campaigning life. I knew that whatever I did I would have to act quickly and in a way which would create media coverage and discussion. I wanted it to be a consciousness raising exercise.

Watching someone I loved dearly die was more traumatic than I realised at the time. It shaped my sense of urgency and a need to intervene. Also I would have to say that the facts do speak pretty much for themselves.

Michael: You say that, but not everyone chooses to start frightening and poisoning innocent people, it seems an odd way to save human beings from themselves.

Barbara: Maybe it was. It didn't seem so at the time. I can't say I haven't had sleepless nights over it since, because I have, but that's not the same as saying that I think I shouldn't have done it. I think I did what I thought was right. To this day I have no answer as to why there wasn't some kind of mass uprising about food right from the start. It baffles me, quite frankly, why people were prepared to kill themselves without a second thought. But that's how it was. There was a strong campaign on behalf of food manufacturers to give the general public a sense that what they were eating was basically good for them. You don't see it now of course, but back then you would go into a supermarket and buy let's say a ready-made sandwich. I used to get so angry. The packaging would make the sandwich look as though it was straight off an organic farmers' market stall, when in reality it was highly processed cheese and meat from usually discarded parts of an animal drenched in an e number concoction given the dubious title of mayonnaise.

The food manufacturers were determined that we should all think this was a healthy option, when it so was not.

Michael: You are suggesting that you really had no faith in the integrity of the supermarket suppliers and manufacturers to keep the general public informed about food?

Barbara: I think I'm saying a lot worse than that actually. The food manufacturers and supermarkets were wilfully keeping information about nutrition away from the general public, and the government of the day colluded with this.

Michael: So it was this belief which led to you making such an extraordinary decision.

Barbara: Absolutely. People are so much better informed these days, but it is worth remembering just where we were. Most of our processed food was laced with hydrogenated fats. Hydrogenated oils have some of the same properties as butter and so are a useful preservative and emulsifier in food. But it's lethal stuff. Hydrogenated oil is oil which has been heated and hydrogen has been passed through it. This gives it the buttery consistency. Hydrogenated fats contain high levels of trans fat. When trans fats cool, they become saturated fat, a type of fat the human body cannot naturally process. It clogs arteries causing cardio-vascular disease and is linked to arthritis. Add to this the horrific findings in a number of research papers concerned with additives. Some additives, still in use I might add, are linked directly to multiple sclerosis and others are thought to cause allergies.

You would be as horrified as I was if you had really taken the time out to read the labels on food. The additives may enhance the colour – if enhancing means making it an unnatural colour. Additives mostly lengthen shelf life. They are not made from substances which are found naturally, they are artificially created. They are allowed because they actually make things taste better to us. Yes, they even enhance the look of a food; maybe even help a bit with the texture – and of course they stabilise the product. They stabilise the product but can harm the person who eats it.

Michael: Barbara, you are incredibly driven; passionate about what you believe in. Where did this drive come from?

Barbara: Where did it come from? That's a really good question. My dad was a railwayman, a keen trade unionist. I suppose I was aware that justice was important as a child and that you could achieve a lot if you could mobilise like-minded people. Where did it come from? Anger. Sheer bloody-mindedness. I think that drove me more than anything else in the end. A lot's talked about grief. You're supposed to go through a cycle of emotions if you are grieving 'properly' – whatever that means. I think I can look back and see that I got stuck on the angry stage of my grieving process.

In time I used the anger constructively. This was an issue not just of ignorance but of a grave injustice. I could see how to change things. I had lost something very precious to me – my quality of life; my family circle – and I guess I needed to make some sense of that. Why me? My answer was why not me – because this change in my life; this change in circumstances if you like, was actually caused to a large degree by others' greed and manipulation – and that in my view had to be stopped.

Michael: Where do you feel this desire to change the world came from?

Barbara: I didn't start out thinking I was changing the world. I started by feeling utterly helpless and in the darkest of rages. I have always been practically minded. I never really thought, even when I was in the thick of the food tampering campaign, that I would do anything more than get people thinking about the topics and get them making their own minds up. In retrospect I can see I was painfully naïve. I thought my attempts to leave messages in food was a bit tame really – and that there was a bigger danger of me being laughed at as some cranky old woman than there was of me being taken seriously.

I wanted the world to be a better place and that was somehow going to redeem, heal if you like, all the pain I had experienced in losing the people I loved. Somehow if I could save a few other people from their clogged arteries or cancer of the colon, then the world would be a bit better place.

I hadn't realised I had so little control over my own anger. Adding washing up liquid and green food colouring to foods was a stupid thing to have done. That only started because I felt the papers weren't taking the initial campaign seriously enough. I didn't ever, for one minute think that other people would get in on the act. I'd felt quite principled about the fact it was my campaign and if I had to suffer as a consequence that was part of the whole process of standing up for what is right.

When the news broke that ground up glass, iron filings and tacks were turning up in food, I got scared. I felt as though I'd opened Pandora's box. I felt entirely responsible – but completely powerless to do anything about it. I tried to find out if any of the well-known eco campaigners were implicated, but they all thought I was nuts even thinking they'd get involved in something so sinister. By then I was confused. Contacting the eco groups was my downfall. The police traced me – and well – I was arrested.

Michael: I have a picture of you as an articulate, driven woman, determined to bring about change pretty much whatever the consequences. What were you like as a child?

Barbara: Probably much the same! I think I was quite a serious little girl. Quite worried what people thought of me. Keen to be seen doing the right thing. I didn't go around hurting my dolls or pulling the legs off spiders or anything gruesome like that if that's what you're thinking! I think I was quite solitary in some ways; a bit inclined to take myself too seriously. I think I probably did think that quite a lot depended on me. It didn't. But I thought it did. You know the sort of thing; if I wasn't nice when we had neighbours over for tea, we wouldn't have a nice tea. Tosh obviously – our neighbours' would have just thought I was a bit of a nuisance I expect.

Michael: At what age did you develop your strong sense of what is right and what is wrong?

Barbara: That's a really difficult one. I think I was always happier knowing where I stood. I thrived with a few rules and regulations – and my mum liked things orderly. I think I became aware of injustice at primary school, when a boy in my class was wrongly accused of stealing something and the boy who had taken the money didn't own up. I knew I wasn't going to be a snitch – but I did go and see our teacher and say that I knew the boy who had been accused hadn't done it and that I knew that someone else had. I was quite annoyed with her response which was to say that unless I was prepared to tell her who had done the crime, she couldn't see what she could do about it. I thought that was really unjust. She should have believed me and freed the other boy from detention.

Michael: Do you think that is where your campaigning drive sprang from?

Barbara: Maybe. I've always been quick to take the underdog's side!

Michael: Do you think your campaigning zeal influenced your choice of career?

Barbara: Yes, I suppose it did. Quite a lot of nursing is to do with supporting people when they feel down, mentally and physically. I did get a buzz out of helping people – but also from teaching people how to take best care of themselves. I've always been very keen on promoting well-being – empowering people. It was funny though, that when it came to the crunch and I needed to empower myself I was hopeless. I could only regain some meaning and purpose in my life by finding an external cause that I could believe in and fight for.

Michael: So to some extent you went into nursing hoping to help people feel good about themselves?

Barbara: I've never looked at it like that, but yes, I think I did.

Michael: Is there any part of you which can now see your decision to sabotage food as a step beyond being helpful to other people?

Barbara: I would be lying if I didn't say that on dark days and some times in the early hours of the morning I do grapple with my conscience and wonder not so much if it was successful – but whether there might have been a better way of achieving the same ends. I can think of ways that might have been more labour intensive and over a much longer time frame could have achieved comparable results, but nothing that could have been as effective as a short sharp shock. Sometimes there isn't a nice, easy option. Sometimes it has to be intense and difficult to have any impact.

Some while ago now, I was contacted by a man who had picked up one of the tampered with packets. He contacted me at the community and was still angry with me as I'd spoiled his love of pork sausages and he thought I was nothing better that some kind of thought police – determined to undermine people's enjoyment of food. He gave me something to think about.

We met not so long ago and I was forced to realise that what I thought had been relatively benign and gentle acts in themselves had not been perceived like that by the victims of the tampering. My intention had been to provoke a thoughtful response and encourage people to think through what they eat and why; have their eyes open and make their choices in the full knowledge of the consequences. In fact what I had done was to frighten and hurt innocent people going about their business, in their own worlds. The chap showed me that my actions had had consequences beyond my wildest imaginings. The last thing I wanted was to make people fearful. My intention had always been to open the debate about choice and inform people about the truth. I just didn't want people dying unnecessarily early. I didn't want to see life wasted.

Michael: Do you feel your own life has not been wasted?

Barbara: Yes I do. On a good day I think I would have the courage of my convictions and do it all again. On a not so good day, I regret the hurt I caused, but not the outcome. The people who were cheating us and feeding us rubbish in more ways than one have been held accountable. That makes the pain, distress and upset well and truly worth it.

Michael: Barbara Dapper, thank you for your honesty and insightfulness into your particularly challenging "Decision Time".

Barbara: Thank you.

Jane Wallman-Girdlestone writes fiction, poetry and Theology. She is also an accomplished fine artist. She is an honorary Fellow in the Divinity School of The University of Aberdeen in Practical Theology, with a special interest in disability and mental health, and the Mission and Ministry Adviser for the Diocese of Moray, Ross and Caithness in The Scottish Episcopal Church. This is Jane's first novel.

She lives in the Highlands of Scotland with her husband. She has three step-children, an adopted son and an extended household menagerie of six dogs and two cats.